Realities: Continental War

The third science fiction/fantasy

novel in the *Realities* trilogy

By Eric Schmiedl

Cover photo illustration by

Creative Works Photography

This book contains coarse language and

depictions of violence and sexuality.

Reader discretion advised.

DISCLAIMER

ABOUT THE AUTHOR

Eric Schmiedl has been a professional writer since 1989, working primarily in print journalism at newspapers in southern Ontario. He is also the author of *Realities* and the memoirs *Don Quixote Versus the Devil* and *South Korean Mania*. He is happily married to Marilyn, to whom he dedicates *Realities: Continental War*.

PROLOGUE

I am Illyad.

My body – my flesh and blood form – was blown to atoms by the weapon my son, Temprus, threw at me all that time ago. It materialized in my chest, exploded, and my body was no more.

I am Illyad.

After that, I was thrown into the great depths of the cosmos. I was left to dwell amongst the planets, the stars ... and more.

I am Illyad.

I have found, in my great travels, that I can manipulate people in different ways than I could before. My ... essence ... can enter other bodies and take them over. I retain my memories and other abilities, along with those of the person I have entered. I can use the person to do my bidding. In tandem with my time-travel powers, I have become more formidable than ever before.

I am Illyad. And the universe is mine for the taking.
All it will take is time.

CHAPTER 1

Circa year 2350 on the distant world Valleria, unwelcome visitor

High Governor Morag sent out a thought message to the other governors of the Council of 11, informing them of the time and location of the next meeting. The location of each meeting varied periodically, rotating amongst governing chambers on the 11 Vallerian continents. The agenda for the meeting would have to come later, but as usual, the environment and space exploration would be hot topics.

"By the Source, I'm tired," Morag thought as she leaned back in her comfortable office chair. It had been a draining week, with everything from political luncheons to protestors at Powers Plaza Triad on the table. And that was just the dealings on Morag's home continent of Vexall … the other governors had been calling for advice on a variety of topics.

Still, all in all, Morag felt good. It had been a productive time for her, with many initiatives being implemented. The most important one, she believed, was the putting in place of air scrubbers throughout the atmosphere of the planet. The air had increasingly become more toxic due to the methane gas being expelled by a growing number of farm animals on Valleria ... the scrubbers sucked in the methane and transformed it to oxygen and nitrogen, making the air much cleaner. In the relatively short time since the scrubber program had been implemented, air quality planetwide had improved by more than 50 per cent.

Morag breathed deeply, her long grey hair flowing around her orange-hued face. Yes, there definitely was progress on many fronts throughout Valleria.

Then, she felt something enter her office. She couldn't see it or hear it but there was certainly something ... someone ... there.

As she prepared to get up from her chair, Morag jerked and fell back. The room went dark for her.

Then, scant minutes later, Morag opened her eyes. But it wasn't just her looking through them. Illyad was looking through them too.

CHAPTER 2

Circa year 1950, peaceful times

Temprus walked the streets of his City, pleased with what he saw. The people of the City had made great progress over the years.

The son of Illyad, Temprus had inherited his father's time-travel powers along with a sense to lead people (although, he noted, he treated people as people, not cattle, as his father had been apt to do). The people of the City loved Temprus, in a way much as they would feel toward a beloved parent.

Even though he had the time-travel powers of his father, Temprus rarely used them, preferring to stay with his Vallerians, to help them grow and prosper. On the odd occasion, he would travel back in time to visit his friends Khamnissa and Whysen, or he would go forward in time to see Dixon Slade. It was interesting so see the past, present and future of the planet Valleria unfold before his eyes. He also kept up on things in the other time eras through his trans-temporal communications device, something he had picked up from his friend from the future, Dixon.

There had not been warfare on Valleria for a long time, since the days of Illyad. This peace was something Temprus cherished. As far as he was concerned, that peace would hold.

Temprus continued walking until he got to his administrative building. He said hello to the person at the front desk and continued on to his office. He sat behind his desk, shuffled through some paperwork (which was something he dreaded) and prepared to start the business of the day.

Then, something happened that hadn't occurred in a while. His trans-temporal device, in a desk drawer, sounded.

"Who could it be?" Temprus wondered. He would soon find out.

CHAPTER 3

Circa year 2150, hope for the future

Dixon Slade had activated his trans-temporal communications device in the hope of contacting his friend from the past, Temprus. Slade was pleased when Temprus answered.

"Hello, friend Temprus," Slade said into the device. "It's a pleasure to talk to you again."

"For me as well, Dixon." Judging by the tone of Slade's voice, it was far from a social call, Temprus thought. "Is all well, Dixon?"

"No, unfortunately," Slade replied. "Our trans-temporal tower has picked up some disturbing action from the future. The temporal activity we detected has the signature of your father's time-travelling abilities, which we recorded years ago. However, they're somewhat different … our technicians can't determine why."

Temprus frowned. His father, back from the dead? It seemed beyond comprehension.

"Dixon, perhaps it's time we met in your era and figured out what is going on. I'll make some preparations in my own time and then I'll make my way to you."

"Excellent. If Illyad is back, as our people fear, we'll need all the help we can get," Slade said.

Slade turned his trans-temporal device to silent mode – he always kept it on in that low-power mode in case of an emergency wherein his allies from other eras wanted to reach him – and sat back in his chair. He had planned to work on civic matters today but this – possible – Illyad matter would take all his concentration for now and, possibly, the near future. At least, that was what Slade thought – indeed, if Illyad had returned, that matter would take all of Slade's time for the foreseeable time to come.

At least, Slade was hopeful there was a future for Valleria. He had the suspicion that if Illyad had come back, the former despot would be more powerful than ever. That thought made Slade shudder.

CHAPTER 4

On a timeless plane, communing

Illyad awoke in a place that was familiar and yet, unreal, at the same time.

"What am I doing here?" Illyad thought.

"I summoned you. I am known as the Entity."

Illyad looked around him but could see nothing but vapour, clouds, and shifting patterns of light. He didn't know what to make of this surreal realm.

"Again, what am I doing here?" Illyad thought.

"I wanted to commune with you. The path you are following, Illyad, can only lead to your destruction. I wanted to show you a different ... a better ... way."

Illyad breathed deeply ... if what he did could actually be called breathing. His lungs were long gone, but his essence could still mimic the act of breathing. He looked around once again but he could not see anything that was capable of speaking, or thinking, in a manner of communing.

"I don't see you … I can only hear you in my mind. This is something I am unfamiliar with, Entity, as you call yourself," Illyad thought.

"No matter. I exist. As do you, although in a manner different than in times past."

Illyad pondered the situation. Would this Entity hinder his plans for Valleria? Could It … or He, or She … end his existence? Illyad would see.

CHAPTER 5

Circa year 2350, civic matters

High Governor Morag awoke as if from a waking dream. It was as though someone had taken over her mind ... her very soul, in fact. She viewed her surroundings, noting everything in her office seemed to be unchanged.

She recalled sending out a thought message to the continental governors but after that, her mind drew a blank. "What happened?" she wondered aloud.

As of yet, only one of the other governors had responded, saying he would be attending the meeting she had called for next week. Although, with this seeming blackout she had suffered, Morag wondered whether she would be better off cancelling the meeting or, at least, postponing it.

Morag got up and looked out the large window that gave her a magnificent view of the Mega-opolis. Its population had grown steeply over the years, and in the past few in particular, causing it to expand in all directions. Some of the people locally had complained to the Mega-opolis councillors about the accompanying loss of agricultural land, and the councillors had sought solutions through farming equipment upgrade subsidies and other initiatives designed to make the most of remaining agricultural territory. That had worked, to a point, but there were still some people in the farming community who remained irked about the course of events.

"Ah well, you can't please everyone," Morag sighed. Although the Mega-opolis farming matters were not directly her problem (even though the planetary seat of leadership was in the Mega-opolis, it was its councillors who dealt with the civic matters here), Morag sympathized with the issues the councillors faced.

Morag made her way back to her office chair. She started to feel light-headed and thought it best to relax. "By the Source?" she said as a strange feeling came over her.

Then, Morag went to sleep and Illyad returned to take over her body. There was plenty of work for him, he reasoned as he opened her eyes once again.

CHAPTER 6

Circa year 2150, feeling of guilt

Temprus clenched his fists and felt himself shift from his own time to that 200 years in the future … the time of Dixon Slade and his contemporaries. Temprus always marvelled at the architecture of 2150, with its gleaming towers and other wonders. Among the towers, air cars moved about freely.

He was a short distance from Slade's offices and he walked towards them briskly. At the front desk, he was greeted by a robot – the front position that had been held by a charming Vallerian the last time Temprus visited this era – and he informed it that he was here to see Slade, the Metropolis head. The robot – which had been told of the time traveller's arrival – smiled, in an artificial way, and directed Temprus to the lift that would take him to Slade.

"What else has changed around here?" Temprus wondered to himself. He was about to see.

The lift stopped and its doors opened, with Temprus just outside of Slade's offices. He came to the appropriate door, put his hand on the imprint reader beside it (his imprint had been added to the computer system some time ago), and the door opened, revealing Slade behind his expansive desk.

Slade smiled.

"Friend Temprus, welcome," Slade said. "It has been too long."

"I agree, Dixon. It's always a pleasure to see you."

Slade motioned to a comfortable chair in front of his desk and Temprus took a seat. The men looked each other squarely in the eye... this would be far more than a simple social call.

"I haven't seen Jack yet, Dixon," Temprus said.

"Ah, my former right hand has retired. Against my wishes, the Metropolis council voted to replace him – and many others – with robots. In my opinion, these contraptions are handy to have around but nothing artificial can replace people like Jack. Ah well, it is the way of things these days. But robots aren't why I contacted you. We've detected temporal activity in the timeline – of a degree not seen since the days of Illyad. I suspect we are seeing the return of your father, as impossible as that might seem."

Temprus looked down. He had always felt a sense of guilt when it came to his father's destruction, which he had brought about personally. He could still see the look on Illyad's face all those years before when the one-time despot realized that his son had tossed a temporal grenade, which a second later detonated in Illyad's chest.

Slade picked up on Temprus' sorrow.

"Ah, I believe you still carry guilt when it comes to Illyad's passing. You shouldn't. Temprus, you simply did what had to be done for the good of Valleria."

"I realize that, Dixon. However, I just can't shake the feeling that I could have dealt with my father differently … perhaps I could have shown him the way to a different, a better, path."

"I sympathize, Temprus. But I insist, there was no other way."

Then, an alert sounded in Slade's office. An alert that signalled someone, or something, very powerful, was travelling in the timeline. Temprus and Slade exchanged worried looks at each other … could this be something they both had dreaded?

CHAPTER 7

Circa year 2150, flash from the future

With a flash of swirling colours, High Governor Morag/Illyad appeared in Dixon Slade's office. Temprus jumped up, fists clenched, while Slade alerted security with the touch of a button on the back of his desk.

"Rest easy, friends," Morag/Illyad said from their muscular, female form. "I am only here to help."

"Who be you?" Temprus asked.

"I am High Governor Morag from the year 2350," the joined persona said. "I understand you have been monitoring timeline activity in my era … for me, it is simply a matter of record." She/he eyed the two men in front of her/him.

"How can we be certain of your identity?" Slade asked. "For all we know, you could be Illyad in disguise."

Morag/Illyad grinned at that. "Of course, if you desire more proof, you shall have it." She/he pulled out a computer record device from their cloak and they showed it to Slade and Temprus. The device showed a variety of records from Morag's time, including such things as the ceremony Morag underwent in her inauguration as high governor of Valleria.

"There is something more I should tell you two," they said. "I am the descendant of Temprus, and Illyad, give or take a couple of hundred years." *"This should throw them off, no doubt,"* Illyad thought from the confines of his mind.

"That would explain your temporal abilities," Temprus said, casting a look at Slade. *"Should they believe this person or not?"* Temprus thought.

For now, Temprus and Slade kept their thoughts to themselves. But they both thought they needed more proof. They would have it in short order.

CHAPTER 8

Circa year 2150-2350, wonders

Illyad, in the body of High Governor Morag, sensed that Dixon Slade and Temprus were hesitant about believing this story of a future high governor of Valleria. They wanted proof, the ex-despot reasoned.

"Come with me to my time ... that should convince you," Illyad/Morag said.

Slade and Temprus looked at each other and nodded. "We'll come with you."

Illyad clenched Morag's left hand into a fist and, suddenly, a swirl of colours surrounded the three bodies in Slade's office. They were transported to 2350 and to Morag's council chamber.

"By the Source," Slade said upon their arrival. The walls of the chamber were made of transparent metals, allowing for a spectacular view of their surroundings. Vallerians seemed to float on by as if they were kept aloft by nothing, again thanks to the transparent materials their crafts were made of. In the background was the familiar mountain range Slade had come to appreciate from the windowed view of his own time.

"Welcome to 2350, gentlemen," Illyad/Morag said. "Can I offer you something to drink?"

Temprus and Slade smiled and nodded and, instantly, two cups of steaming beverages appeared in front of them.

"Our computers can scan your mind and come up with any beverage … pretty much any*thing* … you desire," Illyad/Morag said in explanation. "Just think about something and it becomes reality. In tandem with our fabricators, our computer system has virtually eliminated all want on Valleria. We still have farming, of course, but it's only there more out of tradition – and a desire to taste real vegetables and fruits – than out of necessity."

"Astounding," Temprus said. Even though his temporal powers – when stretched to the limit – would allow him to visit this era on his own, he had never come this far forward in time. It pleased him to see the progress that had been made on his planet.

Slade coughed and turned towards Illyad/Morag.

"These wonders are what one might expect from centuries of advancement," Slade said. "But it is still incredible to see them up close."

"There is more … much more to show you," Illyad/Morag said. "But I grow fatigued – it has been a challenging several days for me. I must rest, but you are welcome to take a guided tour of the city from one of my aides – an android, of course."

Temprus and Slade thanked Illyad/Morag as the joined persona faded to invisibility en route to bed. They would see more of the wonders this era had to offer before heading back to their own respective times.

CHAPTER 9

On a timeless plane, 'pure' goals

Illyad awoke.

"What am I doing here?" he thought.

"It is through me that you are here once again, Illyad. I am the Entity."

"Why have you brought me here this time, Entity?"

"I am curious about what you are doing on Valleria, particularly with High Governor Morag. It is unethical to take over her body without her consent."

"Consent? Do politicians ask consent when they make foolish decisions? I have seen such on Valleria time and again."

The Entity paused. *"And your way is better, Illyad?"*

"My methods might be in question from time to time but my goals are pure. Under my reign, the people of Valleria would benefit greatly in the future."

"Under your reign? Then do you see yourself as a king .... or a dictator?"

It was time for Illyad's essence to pause. *"As I said, my methods ... and how I come to power ... might be questionable by some. But my goals are pure.*

"Perhaps. We shall commune again in a short while, Illyad."

Illyad's essence slept.

CHAPTER 10

Circa year 2350, a nod to the past

Temprus and Dixon Slade waited patiently while the android made its way to them. When they saw it, they noted it looked much like any Vallerian.

"Greetings, gentleman," the android said. "It will be my pleasure to show you around."

"Indeed," Slade said. "And do you have a name?"

"I do," the android replied. "I am Circuit-5."

Temprus smiled. "Well, let's not delay, Circuit-5."

"Of course, sir."

The three of them, with Circuit-5 leading them, made their way to a small hangar where air vehicles were kept. Temprus and Slade could scarcely see them, as they were made of transparent metals, but with Circuit-5's help they hopped aboard one of the vehicles. Circuit-5 stood at the controls of the craft.

"Magnetic beams on this craft, attuned to the metals in your bodies, will hold you in place as we make our way around the Mega-opolis," Circuit-5 said. "You are quite safe."

The two men nodded and the android, deftly touching the controls, made the craft aloft and soon they were riding high above the Mega-opolis.

"You will note the various time eras showing through the architecture," the android told them. "We have tried, as much as possible, to keep the heritage of the various eras intact." Alongside gleaming towers – and some that were scarcely visible except for the lights adorning them – were ancient cathedrals and other such structures.

"I'm happy to see the older buildings," Temprus said, noting that some of the more important structures from his own time were present in the Mega-opolis.

The three of them spent a couple of hours riding above the Mega-opolis before Slade said it was time for them to head back. They would soon have words with High

Governor Morag, who hopefully would be rested enough to talk.

And Illyad would be along for the discussion.

CHAPTER 11

Circa year 2350, ready to talk

Dixon Slade and Temprus thanked Circuit-5 as their craft landed in the Mega-opolis headquarters of High Governor Morag.

"You are quite welcome, gentleman. Let me know if you have any other needs that should be attended to," the android said.

"Can you lead us to the council chambers?" Temprus asked Circuit-5. "It would be best if we waited for the high governor there."

"Of course, sir," the android replied, as she led them to the chambers. "You can wait here for the high governor to arrive. When she awakens, I will ask her to meet you here."

"Excellent," Slade and Temprus said in unison. They each took a seat around the expansive, wooden circle that was the council table.

"Dixon," Temprus said, "so far I haven't seen anything to be alarmed about. Could your instruments have been in error regarding the temporal readings?"

"Impossible, Temprus. I had my people ... er, robots ... triple check the instrumentation before I checked myself. There is definitely something going on here. Whether or not it's Illyad, in some shape or form, is hard to say."

Temprus frowned. "It's just hard for me to believe he could be back. I saw him explode into atoms myself."

"Nonetheless," Slade replied, "it's important that we check things out here before we depart. Just for good measure."

Then, both men turned as Illyad/Morag entered the council chambers.

"Greetings, gentlemen, I am refreshed after my sleep. I am ready for a conversation, if you are," he/she said. Slade and Temprus definitely were up for a talk. Just what they would talk about remained to be seen. The two men from the past wondered just how they would tackle the subject of Illyad's possible return.

CHAPTER 12

Circa year 2350, time to recheck

Dixon Slade decided the direct approach was best.

"High governor," he said before he paused, "I believe Illyad might have, in some shape or form, returned. Just how he has accomplished this is beyond me, however … he was blown apart back in my time, a long time ago."

Morag/Illyad smiled.

"Why do you think this is possible, Dixon?"

"The temporal tracking devices of my time point to Illyad's temporal signature. Unless there is someone with power of the magnitude of Illyad's, I would say the evidence points to him."

It was Morag/Illyad's turn to pause. The joined person thought of something that would throw Slade off track.

"In my time, we have equipment far more advanced … and we have not had similar readings to yours,"

Morag/Illyad said. "Perhaps your instruments are in error."

Slade and Temprus exchanged worried looks. Could they be concerned over nothing?

"High governor," Temprus began, "I find it highly unlikely that the equipment in Dixon's time could be so far off. Have you double-checked your own temporal tracking devices?"

"Of course. They show nothing of the magnitude of temporal power you mentioned. Excuse me, gentlemen, I have a meeting to attend in a few minutes. You are welcome to stay in my time if you want … otherwise, I will bid you goodbye."

Temprus and Slade agreed to return to Slade's time to recheck the temporal devices of that era. This mystery demanded more attention.

Temprus clenched his fists and he and Slade instantly returned to 2150.

CHAPTER 13

Circa year 2150, conflicting information

Dixon Slade had gone over the temporal equipment at his disposal for hours since he and Temprus had travelled to 2150. The two of them had been in Slade's office, accessing everything the computers linked to it had to offer.

"I don't get it, Temprus. Everything checks out … we don't have a problem with the equipment. It definitely recorded power – perhaps Illyad's power, from the levels – some time ago."

Temprus frowned. He didn't like this mystery one bit.

"By the Source, this is confounding," he said. "The information we're receiving here and in the future conflicts."

Slade took another look at the computer information from the vantage point of his large wooden desk – a nod to another, earlier time.

"I can only think of one solution. Morag is lying to us," Slade said.

"I suspected that as well. But why would she do that? What would she have to gain?"

Slade rubbed the stubble on his chin, deep in thought.

"My friend, we have more questions than answers at this point," Slade said. "I think it would be prudent to monitor the situation, see if any more Illyad-type readings emerge, and go forward from there."

"You are right, Dixon. For now, I will return to my own time … but we will keep in contact so you can tell me if the situation changes."

"Very well, Temprus. May all things in your time be peaceful."

With that, Temprus clenched his fists and returned to his own time.

CHAPTER 14

Circa year 1950, return to the past

Illyad's bodiless energy moved through time after leaving High Governor Morag's body in a coma, that he had induced, in her quarters. That way, he reasoned, she could not circumvent any of his plans – even if she were aware of them, which he assured himself she could not be.

"I am entering my son's time period," Illyad thought as his energy descended on Temprus' City. It looked much larger than in the days when Illyad himself had governed here, the bodiless being thought.

Illyad viewed the people in the streets in the midday Source's light until he came across one he wanted to enter – a big, strapping man with bronzed orange skin. This one would be suitable to the former dictator's needs.

"Ah yes," the now embodied/joined man said as they breathed air deeply into their lungs. The man whom

Illyad had entered was named Jonas and he was a tradesman, which in part explained his muscular frame. Illyad/Jonas flexed the muscles in that frame, relishing in the feeling of physical power.

From there, the joined man decided on a course of action. They would seek out Temprus' offices and see if Illyad's son was available to talk. Illyad had missed seeing Temprus from that time in the future when the ex-despot had inhabited Morag's form.

It seemed the City's administrative seat had remained in basically the same spot as when Illyad governed here so long ago. For Illyad, it was both a second and a millennium ago. Illyad/Jonas walked up the steps to the City's government reception area and told the clerk who met them that they would like to speak to Temprus.

"Ah, what little has changed in this structure," the joined man said to himself as he waited. Soon, the wait bore fruit as Temprus emerged from behind a large wooden door.

"Greetings, my friend," Temprus said, extending his hand. "And your name is?"

"Jonas. We have much to talk about."

CHAPTER 15

Circa year 2150, power emerges

Dixon Slade sat in his office, working at the civic matters of the Metropolis. He had led the massive municipality for a long time and it seemed as though the work involved with it never ended.

On his computer screen, document after document flashed by. There would be dozens – hundreds of them – to go through by the end of the day.

"Time to check in on the home front," Slade said to himself after a couple of hours had passed. He pressed a button and put in a call to his wife, Melissa.

"Hello Dixon," Melissa's image said as it floated above his desk. "Still keeping busy at the office, I trust?"

"Of course, dear," he said with a smile. "I thought I'd check in with you and to tell you that I love you more each day."

The couple talked for a while longer, bantering about their respective days, until an alarm buzzed in Slade's office. Its source was the trans-temporal equipment that Slade had installed all those years ago.

"Sorry dear, I must go. I'll see you soon," Slade said.

"All right, Dixon. I'll see you tonight," Melissa said before her image flickered into nothingness.

From his computer, Slade called up the report behind the alarm. Its results made his eyebrows rise. The report indicated that power equivalent to Illyad's had emerged in yet another time.

It was from the 1950s era – Temprus' time.

"By the Source," Slade said under his breath. It was time to put in a call to 1950.

CHAPTER 16

Circa year 1950, a mystery

Temprus sat behind his desk, looking at Illyad/Jonas. This man seemed somewhat familiar to the City leader, although he couldn't quite say why.

"So, Jonas, you are new to our City, is that right?"

"That's correct. I come from the Highlands and am here to make a better life for myself and my family. I have two daughters and they like the City very much."

"Ah, that's great ... a family man."

Illyad/Jonas thought back to the time when Temprus had destroyed Illyad's body with a trans-temporal grenade. Even so, Illyad thought, he continued to love his son Temprus as much as when he was just born.

"I was looking for employment opportunities upon my arrival in the City," Illyad/Jonas continued, "and I thought my trade skills might gain me a job. I am a craftsman, making intricate pieces of ironworks."

"I think you will find our City accommodating, Jonas. Let me talk to my assistant about some possible employment avenues you can pursue. Excuse me a moment." Temprus left the office to speak to his assistant, leaving Illyad/Jonas to think.

"I do believe the City has grown markedly," Illyad thought. *"I will do well here."*

A few minutes passed and Temprus returned with a sheet of paper.

"Jonas, here's a list of possible employers. Of course, you might think about starting your own business … we have programs to help you."

"Thank you, Temprus. I'll be on my way." With that, Illyad/Jonas extended a hand in greeting and left the office.

"A nice man," Temprus thought to himself as Illyad/Jonas left.

Then, Temprus heard his trans-temporal communications device going off. He answered.

"Temprus, it's Dixon. My equipment has tracked the temporal signature of Illyad – or somebody with power similar to his – to your time."

"To my time? By the Source." The two agreed to meet in Slade's era to unravel the mystery.

CHAPTER 17

On a timeless plane, thoughts of conquest

The Entity summoned Illyad.

"I have observed you in Temprus' time," the Entity thought. *"What are your intentions toward your son?"*

Illyad paused before replying.

"I do believe my son has done an admirable job in building up my City. However, I also believe I could do better."

"In what way?"

"Through conquest, I could build the City up into something even grander."

"But through peaceful means, Temprus has done an admirable job – as you said - with the City. Why must you turn to conquest to change things?"

Again, Illyad paused before thinking in reply.

"With added resources, which can be most quickly gained by taking over neighbouring communities, the City would grow exponentially."

"I believe a slow and steady progression would be best," the Entity replied. *"Your plan would lead to countless deaths, which has been your pattern in the past."*

"I disagree with you. Progress, through any means possible – including through warfare – is desirable. In the end, I would do far more good than harm."

"No. It is wrong."

"Who are you to question my methods?"

"I am the Entity. That is all that need be said."

"Will you stop me?"

"No. I am against direct interference, whether it be on Valleria or elsewhere. But at some point, I feel compelled to convince you against your intended course of action." It was the Entity's turn to pause. *"Return to*

Valleria for now ... we will converse again at some point."

CHAPTER 18

Circa year 2150, on the alert

Temprus materialized in Dixon Slade's time and near Slade's Metropolis government headquarters. He got his bearings and began to walk to Slade's offices.

"By the Source, how did that temporal signature make its way to my time?" Temprus wondered to himself as he approached Slade's office door. The door opened automatically, revealing Slade at his desk.

"Hello, friend Dixon," Temprus said. Slade nodded in reply and motioned Temprus to have a seat in the comfortable chair in front of the desk.

"Temprus, there's no mistaking it. The temporal signature we monitored in 2350 has emerged in your time."

"Can you pinpoint the signature?"

"Our equipment isn't that precise, at least not at this time. But, trust me, the signature has appeared in your era."

Temprus leaned back in the chair with a frown on his face. Could it be his father Illyad, back from the dead? Knowing Illyad, anything was possible, Temprus reasoned to himself.

"Dixon, I'm at a loss. It is a signature that matches that of Illyad but we saw him blown to atoms … could his – for lack of a better word - spirit be roaming the eras of Valleria?"

"I don't know. But we are both well aware of the powers Illyad exhibited in the past. I'm certain we're dealing with a very powerful being, whether it be Illyad or someone with powers similar to his."

Both men sighed, looking each other in the eye. At length, Slade spoke.

"We'll have to continue monitoring the situation, Temprus. All I know is that this being – Illyad or not –

deserves our full attention. When this being uses his, or her, powers, we'll be able to, at least, know what era he or she is in."

"That's reassuring, Dixon. But I won't be sleeping too soundly for the next while nonetheless."

"You and I both."

The men spoke for a while longer before Temprus returned to his own time to tend to government affairs. But in the back of his mind, he would be on the alert at all times.

CHAPTER 19

Circa year 1950, woman of the night

Illyad/Jonas walked the streets of the City, intent on finding a woman of the night. It had been too long since the former dictator had had the company of a woman, he reasoned, and it was high time for it.

"The City has grown considerably since I was last here," the joined being thought. *"But some things never change."*

The joined being continued their walk, looking up and down the back alleys. Eventually, they found what they were looking for, in a scantily-clad woman whose name was Trina.

"Hello handsome," she said to Illyad/Jonas. "What brings you to this part of town?"

"You, my dear."

"Smooth talker, and muscular, too. I like that in a man."

"Is there somewhere we can go where it's a bit quieter? I have the need for a bit of silence," the joined being said.

"Of course. I have a little place, just around the corner, that should meet your needs," Trina replied.

They walked together for a short distance until Trina motioned to a green door in the centre of a brown-brick wall. She unlocked the door and she and the joined being entered. Once inside, she turned on a light.

"Time to get down to business, wouldn't you say?" the woman uttered in a seductive tone.

"Yes, my dear, I certainly agree," he said, motioning to the bedroom.

The two bodies made love for hours, with her moaning and screaming as Jonas/Illyad enjoyed the sex as if had been years since the last time the joined being had intercourse – and for Illyad, that was particularly true.

Lying on the bed, Trina turned to the joined being and smiled.

"Now it's time to discuss payment."

"Of course, my dear. It is indeed time to give you your due." With that, Illyad/Jonas reached for their clothes, pulled a dagger out from underneath them and plunged it into Trina's heart. Blood spurted across the room as a look of shock and horror crossed her face.

"Prostitutes," the joined being said, "deserve nothing better than death." Illyad/Jonas grinned, watching the blood flow.

Then, the joined being got out of bed and dressed. They had been careful to ensure none of the blood remained on them.

"Farewell, my dear. Have a pleasant stay in eternity."

CHAPTER 20

Circa year 2350, introducing Ting

Illyad's essence moved through Valleria's timelines before arriving back in the year 2350. He had left Jonas' body in a comatose state back several hundred years ago, until Illyad wanted to make use of it again.

"It is time I took control of things here once again," Illyad thought, before arriving at High Governor Morag's quarters. She lay in a comatose state, identical to that of Jonas, awaiting Illyad's return. Illyad's essence entered her body and the joined being of himself and Morag awoke.

"Ah, it is good to be back in power," Illyad thought, through the synapses of Morag's brain. The Morag half of the joined being continued to lie dormant, unaware of what was going on. But the Illyad half? Ah, that was another matter entirely.

Mentally, Illyad drafted a rough draft of a thought message he wanted to pass on to the heads of Valleria's

11 continents. He wanted a meeting of them as soon as possible. Just what he had in mind was hard to pinpoint, as he himself was unsure of his future steps in becoming supreme ruler of Valleria in this time period. This meeting would be more of a fact-finding mission – to determine the characters of the continental leaders and who could be coaxed into following him down the road.

Illyad/Morag got up, got dressed and exited the quarters. The thought message could wait for a few moments. Illyad realized the body he inhabited required food and water after its slumber, awaiting his return. The joined being made its way to a nearby food dispensary, made a selection of sustenance, and ate and drank.

"It feels good to have food and water going down my – Morag's – throat," Illyad thought. He savoured the feeling. After eating and drinking, the joined being continued on his/her way to Morag's high governor office situated in the Mega-opolis. There, Illyad could review the thought files in Morag's brain in silence, which is what he preferred for such things.

The joined being sat behind Morag's desk, reflecting on the files. Of all those available, the ones that most intrigued him were those pertaining to Ting, the governor of the northernmost continent of Makown. This was for a number of reasons: Ting was the least diplomatic of leaders on a planet made up of, primarily, diplomats. He governed with relatively fierce economic policies, spending the least on social services and the most on the military per capita of all the governors. Also, he had a reputation for being something of a gambler, womanizer, and drinker.

"Indeed," Illyad grinned with Morag's mouth, "this gentleman reminds me a little bit of myself.

The meeting of all the governors could wait. Illyad wanted to meet Ting one-on-one first.

CHAPTER 21

Circa year 2350, rule by fear

Makown Governor Ting (many also referred to him as Supreme Leader of the Makown continent and he preferred that title, if the truth were to be known) walked around his immaculate gardens behind his palace. He kept a scowl on his face despite the pleasant day and watched his gardeners as they toiled in the dirt. They were very aware of Ting's presence and worked diligently lest they incur his legendary wrath.

"Ah, the smells, the sights, of the plants please me," Ting said to no one in particular. He touched one of the flowers, bringing it up to his face to take in its fragrance. Many regarded his love of plants to be contradictory to the rest of the man: At once, he could love plants and hate his fellow Makownians (and indeed, all of the populace of Valleria).

Ting craved power and most of it that he held now in Makown was handed down through a family dynasty. However, his father – who had ruled the continent with a kind, gentle hand – was day compared to Ting's night. The populace of Makown regarded Ting's rule as the worst time in the continent's history. He spent little on the people themselves, instead putting funds into an enormous military budget that made Makown the most feared area on all of Valleria.

He continued walking, going from plant to plant, until he felt hungry. Then, he went to a tree and picked one of the fruits from a low-leaning branch. He revelled in the sweetness of the fruit's flesh. As he chewed, he walked towards the massive palace and entered. From there, he made his way to his personal office, passing by the armed guards who continuously stood by there.

Going behind his desk, he snapped his fingers and a screen appeared, highlighting the day's reports from various locales of the continent.

"Ah, good, the mining of the western hills is going on as planned," Ting thought to himself. The hills were rich in precious ores and he wanted as much as he could get to boost his coffers, and in turn, his military. Without

huge funding, his military machine would collapse – his armed forces were made up mainly of mercenary leaders who kept the rank and file in line.

He continued to scan the reports, with varying expressions crossing his face (but always changing back to his default scowl). Most of the reports pleased him, however, and his disposition was – for him – relatively pleasant. Then, he heard a chime that signalled someone was coming to see him. It was one of his staff.

"Sir, I have a thought message from High Governor Morag. Should I transfer it to you?"

"Yes," he replied simply. The staff member closed her eyes, thought for a moment, and the message went to Ting.

"That will be all," he said, and the staffer left his presence quickly. She was obviously intimidated by Ting and she was all too happy to exit.

"Ah, we'll see what this bitch wants," Ting thought to himself of Morag. He had always hated her after she was

voted in as planetary leader by the Council of 11 – of course, in the council election for leader in which he had been soundly defeated, he had lobbied to become the head of Valleria himself. The other, peace-loving continent heads had held a different view.

The message wasn't quite what Ting had expected.

CHAPTER 22

Circa year 2350, an eye on domination

Illyad/High Governor Morag sat at the head of the Council of 11 meeting room. He/she was alone and Illyad was preparing for the coming meeting with Makown Governor Ting. The head of Makown had agreed to a meeting – on his own terms, and on his own turf, the next day.

"This man bears some investigating," Illyad thought to himself. *"I want to know more about him."* He began the long process of delving into Morag's memories, going through the synapses of her brain in the process.

"Interesting," Illyad thought.

As Illyad had already thought, Ting was a force to be reckoned with (although he paled in comparison with Illyad himself, the former dictator of Valleria thought). Ting had been in power for quite some time – indeed, it had been decades since the then-teenage Ting had become ruler of Makown. Ting's father had died under mysterious circumstances and many had suspected that Ting himself was responsible for the death of the father.

Upon becoming head of Makown, Ting was a merciless leader, executing his detractors with regularity and ferocity. He had made those executions public, to serve as a warning to others that he was not to be fooled with. In the early days, there had been uprisings against Ting but he put them down as quickly as they had arisen.

Ting liked his women, to say the least. Even though he had been married early in his career, as Makownian custom had called for, Ting had gone through a slew of concubines and prostitutes, discarding each of them as quickly as he had taken them on. And he was known as a legendary gambler – not only did he frequent casinos on occasion, accompanied by his ever-present armed guards, he had tried to make wagers of power and trade with the heads of neighbouring continents. For example, he would make wagers of precious ores against a neighbour's technological advances or vast amounts of lumber, with games of chance deciding the victor. The other continental heads didn't go for these games, much to Ting's chagrin.

When it came to looking after his people, Ting, quite simply, did as little as possible. When workers on his continent became too old to labour, Ting just let them fend for themselves. Disabled people were shunned on his continent, left to beg or simply die if they couldn't find a way to support themselves.

And Ting's military was second to none on Valleria, due to his enormous military budget. Indeed, Illyad thought, Ting had the potential to rule all of the planet, even though he lacked the courage to risk the final steps to global domination.

"This man seems like he was handed the way to global power from an early age, yet he lacks the will to do what's necessary to conquer his peers and make Valleria a better place for all – in the long run," Illyad thought.

"What this man lacks, I have," Illyad continued. *"Perhaps I will show him my way of doing things, then*

rip the power from him. It will only take some time. I
look forward to tomorrow's meeting."

CHAPTER 23

Circa year 2350, planting suspicions

Illyad/High Governor Morag appeared near Ting's palace. The modified wormhole technology of Valleria – a byproduct of the ongoing early exploration of space – made it easy to go from one part of the planet to another.

"This is quite an impressive headquarters," Illyad/Morag thought. Although Morag had dealings with Governor Ting on a regular basis, this was the first time her eyes had set sight on Ting's palace.

The joined being saw Ting – flanked by armed guards – approaching.

"Greetings," Ting said cordially. "I was surprised to receive your message, high governor. We have never met face to face on my home soil.

"This meeting was long overdue," Illyad/Morag said. "I am trying to make the rounds with all my governors, to get firsthand updates on their varied situations."

Ting and the joined being – with the guards in tow – walked through the palace gardens at length, talking about world affairs. Illyad/Morag said they were pleased with the strides made technologically in the past decade, while looking forward to future developments.

"Yes, weaponry has come a long way," Ting remarked, which made the joined entity grin.

"This man will be all I need to pave my way to power over Valleria," Illyad thought in the back of Morag's mind.

"Speaking of weaponry, you will surely need it in the years – nay, months – ahead," Illyad/Morag said.

"Why do you say that?" Ting asked.

"I have heard rumblings of dissent among your neighbouring continents. They fear you will start a war in the near future and they are contemplating a pre-emptive strike – to cripple you while they can. I am breaching confidentiality laws by telling you this but I thought you had a right to know."

Ting's eyebrows shot up.

"Thank you for telling me this. My forces will be on high alert until I can verify your claims of conflict," Ting said.

Illyad/Morag grinned again. *"The fool. It will be all to easy to plant evidence for him."*

CHAPTER 24

Circa year 1950, murder investigation

Temprus went for a walk in the early morning light. He liked to stretch his legs before making his way to the City offices and this morning was no exception.

"Ah, a beautiful day," Temprus thought as he rounded several blocks. All was tranquil in the City at this early hour, although that would soon change.

Temprus eventually headed home to prepare for the day. A quick shower and breakfast and he was ready to leave for the office. Upon his arrival there, an ashen-faced assistant met him.

"Sir, there's been a murder in the City. A woman named Trina."

Temprus was shocked. Ever since his father Illyad had become history in the City, murder within its confines was virtually unknown. Indeed, this would go down as the first murder in the history of the City police department, which was formed a quarter-century ago.

"This is terrible. I'm going to police headquarters to look into this myself," Temprus told the assistant.

Police Chief Stapper was talking to the local news organizations about the murder when Temprus arrived at police headquarters. Stapper was fielding questions about the death during a press conference.

"We have no suspects at this time," Stapper, a broad-shouldered man with close-cropped hair, said in response to one of the queries. He continued to respond to additional questions for close to 20 minutes before cutting the press conference short.

"I must continue the investigation before I can tell you anything further," Stapper said in finality. Then, he turned to Temprus.

'If you can step inside with me, Temprus, I can talk to you further about what you missed," the police chief said. The two men went inside to Stapper's office.

"At this point, sir, we are following up on leads but we don't have anything too solid yet. This investigation is very young."

"How was the woman killed?"

"By a single stab wound. We have yet to find the murder weapon."

"Has her family been notified?"

"As far as we know, she had no immediate family, although we're looking into that further. She was, however, a known prostitute. My people have had several dealings with her over the years. She basically kept to herself when she wasn't ... working, so to speak."

Temprus frowned. "Anything else?"

"Not at this point. I'll keep you updated as the investigation unfolds."

"Please do. Thanks, chief. I'll be at City Hall if you need me."

Temprus left the headquarters. This would be a day marked in infamy in the City.

CHAPTER 25

Circa year 2150, meeting on the way

Dixon Slade looked at the latest findings from the long-range temporal equipment. There was no mistaking it ... the powerful time-travel readings were now coming from the future.

"I'll have to keep monitoring this. Damn, I wish I knew for sure what was causing these temporal readings," Slade thought to himself. He decided to maintain monitoring for the moment but, if these off-the-scale reports continued, it might be time to contact Temprus and make another visit to 2350.

For now, though, his hands were full with Metropolis business. There was trouble brewing on his council, with some of the members voicing the opinion that the temporal programs that Slade had pushed for, for so long, should be scrapped. These councillors were arguing that Slade and his staff – much of it robotic, admittedly - had enough to keep them occupied in this era. They had no business dealing with other times, these members said. If their wishes came to fruition, everything having to do with temporal equipment – including the trans-temporal tower, the heart of the time program – would be history.

"That just won't do," Slade thought to himself. *"I've worked too hard for this to see it come to an end."*

Perhaps a meeting with his deputy on council, Curtis Trelane, was in order, Slade reasoned. Trelane – who should have been Slade's right-hand man – was instead leading the charge for the dismantling of the temporal program. Slade sent a message to Trelane, requesting a private meeting.

Minutes turned into hours as Slade waited for a response. At long last, the Metropolis head's computer screen lit up with an image of Trelane.

"Greetings, Curtis. I appreciate your getting back to me."

"Indeed, Dixon. I had some matters to attend to before returning your message. How can I help you?"

"I would like to meet with you, in my office if that's all right with you. We have some things to discuss."

Trelane smiled. He had a pretty good idea of what the meeting would be about ... the matter of trans-temporal technology had been discussed at length in recent council meetings.

"Of course, Dixon. Would tomorrow morning be soon enough?"

"Definitely. I'll be in my office all day. You can come when you like."

"Then I'll see you in the morning." Trelane's image disappeared from the computer screen, signalling the end of the conversation.

Slade sat back in his chair. He looked forward to tomorrow's meeting.

CHAPTER 26

Circa year 2350, fuming

Makown Governor Ting strode with heavy feet in the gardens surrounding his palace headquarters. High Governor Morag had left just over an hour ago and Ting continued to fume over what she had told him.

"Wage war? With me? The other governors must be mad. In an armed conflict, I would crush them into powder," Ting thought.

Still, the idea of a military strike against the Makown continent made Ting's blood boil. He continued striding through the gardens, their beauty lost on him at the moment.

Ting, with his armed guards a few paces behind him, walked to the opening of his palace office. The guards stopped at the entrance while Ting went into the office to mull things over. Should he contact the other governors about this? No, he reasoned, it would be a sign of weakness on his part and they might strike against him all the sooner.

"The bitches and bastards," Ting thought of his fellow governors. *"They won't get the best of me."*

Ting began sending out private thought messages to some of his key staff members, particularly to his head of security. It would be prudent to do some digging behind the scenes, to see just how prepared his continental neighbours were to attack him.

Ting went to the bar he kept well-stocked in his office and poured himself a drink. It would settle him down.

"Ah, that's good," Ting said to himself after he downed his drink. He set the glass down and mentally reviewed the news of the day from the nearest continents. Nothing seemed to stand out on the various newscasts.

"That means nothing," Ting thought to himself. *"These cowards are hiding behind closed doors, making their plans ... I'm sure of it."*

And while Ting fumed, Illyad grinned half a world away. The former dictator didn't know exactly what Ting was thinking but he could be sure that the Makown governor was planning ... planning what?

His own destruction, in the long run. Illyad grinned again.

CHAPTER 27

Circa year 1950, waiting for the word

City Police Chief Stapper continued to read through reports pertaining to Trina's murder. His office had received several tips about the killing already, although the investigation into the death was in its infancy. This type of crime continued to make his stomach churn, particularly since this was the first murder he had dealt with.

"I wonder what the motive was ... nothing was missing from the woman's apartment. That rules out robbery. Was this simply a random act of violence?" Stapper thought.

Then, a call came in. The caller didn't identify herself.

"If you want to catch the killer, you'd best look into the background of a tall, broad-shouldered fella living in the Jonora district." The caller continued to detail the man she was talking about, talking about his long dark hair and fair complexion. The man was fairly handsome, she continued, before hanging up.

Stapper leaned back in his chair and pondered the call. This could be nothing, of course, but he couldn't afford not to look into it. He called for one of his detectives – when he arrived, Stapper ordered him to the Jonora district, armed with the description Stapper had received from the caller.

"Be discrete," Stapper told the detective before the latter left. "I don't want the killer being alerted to this tip."

Next, Stapper called Temprus. The City leader had asked Stapper to keep him informed about the investigation and the chief was following that instruction to the letter.

"Yes, Temprus, we're looking into the tip now. But it could take some time before anything solid materializes."

"By the Source, this whole affair is unnerving," Temprus replied. "How are you holding up?"

"I'm fine. But I think some of my people are anxious. They've never dealt with a murder."

"They should have been around in my father's time. Then, there was enough death going around to satisfy even the most morbid of tastes."

"Yes, I know something of those days. Terrible. I'll keep you up to date on the investigation."

After the call was complete, Stapper leaned back in his chair, awaiting word from the detective. It would take a while before that word came.

CHAPTER 28

On a timeless plane, a better way?

The Entity summoned Illyad.

"You are here to talk to me about the woman you killed, as well as your dealings with Governor Ting," the Entity thought. *"I know your intentions with the latter but I want you to tell me why the woman had to die."*

"She was a common prostitute and deserved nothing better."

"There were reasons why she chose that path. Indeed, the path might have chosen her."

Illyad paused. *"No matter. It is done. And I would do the same again and likely will do the same again."*

It was the Entity's turn to pause. Then, the Entity thought.

"Also, is there not a better way to live than by taking over the bodies of others? They don't deserve to be your puppets."

"What other way is there?"

"You could inhabit an android form and live a long and fruitful life. You wouldn't have to ruin others' lives that way."

"That would prevent me from seeking power on Valleria – when I take over High Governor Morag, I gain her political standing – and stop me in my quest to make things better on the planet for all the populace."

"I can see you aren't ready to commune with me at this time. We will meet again later ... return to Valleria for now."

CHAPTER 29

Circa year 2150, a civil meeting

Dixon Slade sat behind his desk, waiting for the arrival of Curtis Trelane. Slade was both apprehensive about this meeting while looking forward to it.

Then, the buzzer sounded, signalling he had a visitor. The door to the office opened via Slade's telekinesis – he still found a use for his power from time to time – and, shortly after, in walked Trelane.

"Greetings, Dixon," the slight of build Trelane said. "I imagine we should get right down to business, if that's fine with you."

"Of course, Curtis. Please, have a seat. Would you like some coffee?"

"Definitely, thank you." The two men were being more than civil to each other in this prelude to business.

One of Slade's robots brought coffee in for the two men and they sat and sipped their beverages. Then, Trelane spoke.

"Dixon, you know where I stand when it comes to our trans-temporal programs. I think our best interests are focused on our time, not dealing with time emanations from other eras. Besides, we don't have the technology as of yet to travel to those eras, so what's the point of keeping tabs on them in this fashion?"

"I believe you're making my point. If we continue with the temporal programs, they will eventually pay off in giving us the ability to time travel. And keeping up to date with temporal emanations from other eras keeps us current … indeed, we can prepare for possible threats to our security by monitoring different points in time."

Trelane looked thoughtful. Then, at length, he spoke.

"I believe that *you* believe these programs are worthwhile, Dixon. However, I'm not convinced. We should take this up with the entire council at our next meeting."

"Of course. Maintaining these programs should go before council. I, for one, will be adamant that they should continue."

"And I will take the opposing view. I hope that doesn't upset you personally."

"It doesn't. Thank you for coming in, Curtis."

The men finished their coffee and Trelane left shortly thereafter, leaving Slade to ponder the future of the trans-temporal programs he had worked so hard for.

CHAPTER 30

Circa year 1950, talking to the press

Temprus fielded yet another call from one of the local newspapers about Trina's death. He spoke to them briefly – he couldn't talk about the tip, lest he give away too much of the ongoing investigation – and, after the call was over, pondered the possibility of holding a press conference the following day. That might satisfy the curiosity of the press corps, while giving Police Chief Stapper the opportunity to appeal to the public for further clues.

"By the Source, this is something I hope I don't have to deal with again in the future," Temprus thought from behind his office desk.

As important as this murder investigation was to his administration, there were other, more mundane things to deal with for the time being. Reports had to be read on civic matters of various description and Temprus had an upcoming meeting with his advisers that he had to prepare for. Before those issues were dealt with, though,

Temprus thought it best to phone Stapper and propose the press conference.

"Greetings, Temprus," Stapper said when the City leader called. "We're still busy looking up some tips – more have come in – and I'm waiting to hear from my people about the goings on in the Jonora district."

"That's good to hear, chief. What say you about organizing a press conference regarding the murder ... let the public know what's happening and appeal for further leads into Trina's murder," Temprus replied.

"I think you're correct in wanting a press conference, although I'm not sure we're ready for it yet. Perhaps give me a day to think about it," Stapper said.

"Good enough, chief. Keep me posted and I'll do the same for you."

As the call ended, it occurred to Temprus that, perhaps, his time travel powers could be of aid in solving the murder. Could he go back to the time of the killing and actually witness it? Indeed, that could solve the matter.

Temprus leaned back in his chair and smiled. He wondered why he hadn't thought of this before.

But better late than never.

CHAPTER 31

Circa year 2350, playing games

Illyad's essence floated through time and space before, once again, inhabiting High Governor Morag's body. He noted it was like putting on an old, familiar set of gloves. He was becoming used to inhabiting her.

Illyad/Morag grinned. Now was the time to continue setting things in motion.

Striding to the Council of 11 chambers, he/she took the high seat of power. From here, it would be easy to relay thought messages to the other council members.

"I hereby convene a meeting of the Council of 11," he/she thought. *"I ask you all to attend in the Mega-opolis council chambers in three days from now."*

The joined being waited, then waited some more. Eventually, return messages trickled back into Illyad/Morag's brain. First one, then another, of the continental governors returned the message, saying they would attend. Ultimately, only Makown Governor Ting was absent from the list of attendees.

"I'll give him some more time," the joined being thought. *"The fun is just beginning, I'm sure of it."*

At long last, Ting responded, thinking that he was far too busy to attend. However, he would let Morag know whether he could free up his schedule and make the meeting.

"That's not a surprise," Illyad/Morag thought. *"I'm sure he'll come; he just wants to play games at this point."*

The joined being leaned back in the comfortable chair at the head of the Council of 11 table. He/she grinned.

"Let him play his games," he/she thought. *"I'm better at it than Ting."*

CHAPTER 32

Circa year 1950, view to a kill

Temprus clenched his fists, propelling him back through time. Rather than go back centuries as he had done in the past, he merely moved back days ... back to the day, to be precise, of Trina's murder.

Temprus walked the streets of the City. He had come back earlier in the day than he had planned and so had some time to kill. He went into a coffee shop, ordered his drink, and then took a seat at one of the orange-topped tables and nursed his beverage. After a while, he picked up one of the newspapers out of the rack at the side of the shop and indulged himself with what was, to him, old news.

"I had forgotten about that one," he said aloud as he re-read a story about a mother in the City delivering quintuplets. "I wonder how she's doing now?"

After he finished his coffee, Temprus eyed the door of the shop. Perhaps it was time to make his way to Trina's apartment, he thought to himself.

Temprus left the shop and made his way to the area where Trina lived. He didn't want to be late, lest he miss the chance to reveal the identity of Trina's killer. Minutes later, he was standing across the road from Trina's apartment.

"I'd best stay to the shadows, so the killer can't see me," Temprus thought. He positioned himself in an alleyway, out of view of the people on the street outside the apartment.

Eventually, the Source began to set, signalling dusk. Temprus waited patiently as the minutes, then hours, crept by.

Then, while Temprus kept his eyes open to view the killer, Trina and a tall man appeared at the end of the street. As they drew closer to the apartment, Temprus gasped.

The man with her was Jonas.

CHAPTER 33

Circa year 2350, seeds of war

Illyad/High Governor Morag sat at the head of the Council of 11. Everyone on the council had taken their places at the massive, horseshoe-shaped table with the exception of Makown Governor Ting.

"Thank you all for coming," the joined being said to the other governors in attendance. "It is time we get started."

There were the usual housekeeping items to contend with. However, before long, the governors' collective attention was turned to the absence of Ting and the rumours of war that had started circulating among the continents.

"This is outrageous," Jackoo Governor Rollins said at last. "If Ting wants war, let's give him war." Jackoo was the closest continent to Makown and Rollins was particularly irate about the prospect of his larger neighbour starting a conflict.

"Calm yourself," the joined being said. "War would solve nothing at this point in our history. Peace is our way."

However, even though the joined being preached peace, Illyad grinned internally at the prospect of conflict.

"Ah, I can hear the drums of war beating already," Illyad thought. *"War is all but inevitable, to be sure."*

Even as Illyad inwardly thought of conflict, the joined being continued to preach peace. But the seeds of war had been planted.

CHAPTER 34

Circa year 2150, pacing

Dixon Slade paced in his office. After his meeting with Curtis Trelane, he continued to worry about the fate of the trans-temporal program. He had put too much time and resources into the program to see it fade away.

"Damn that man," Slade thought. *"He could ruin the entire program if I'm not careful."*

He continued to pace, gathering his thoughts, until a familiar chime sounded. It was the latest temporal report. Slade looked up at the screen on the wall as it came to life, showing the report.

There had been numerous readings pointing to Illyad's temporal signature. These emerging readings had come from the past, as well as the future, recently. It was definitely a cause of concern for Slade.

"If he's playing games back and forth in time, it's only a matter of days – perhaps hours – before he shows up in this temporal period," Slade said to himself. "It's something we'll have to take seriously."

There were reports to be done on the civic front, Slade noted, but those would have to wait. It was imperative that Illyad be dealt with – if it were, indeed, Illyad causing this temporal activity.

It was time to use the trans-temporal communications device and speak with Temprus.

CHAPTER 35

Circa year 1950, information

Temprus clenched his fists and returned to his own time. He was still fighting a feeling of disbelief … Jonas the murderer? He had seemed to Temprus to be a fine, upstanding citizen of the City. However, Temprus thought to himself, he had only seen Jonas with Trina outside her apartment – it wasn't proof that Jonas was the killer. Even so, Temprus would report what he had seen to Chief Stapper.

It was midday and Temprus saw The Source high in the Vallerian sky, and he was soaking in its rays on his orange skin as he made his way to police headquarters. Things were relatively quiet as the investigation into Trina's death made slow headway. Well, that would pick up a bit with this piece of news, Temprus thought.

"Hello, I'm here to see Chief Stapper," Temprus told the clerk at the front of the police offices. The clerk motioned the City leader to Stapper's office.

"Greetings, Chief," Temprus said upon seeing Stapper. "You and I have to talk."

"That's fine, Temprus. What's on your mind?"

Then, Temprus explained how he had made a comparatively short trip back in time and that he had seen Jonas with Trina on the eve of her murder. Stapper looked surprised.

"I've heard nothing but good things about Jonas," Stapper said. "He's a fine example of citizenship … volunteers for everything, including the police auction. Did you actually see him commit the crime?"

"No, I only saw him with Trina on the night of her murder. It's not a guarantee that he committed the crime, to be sure, but it is pretty damning."

"Well, I'll dispatch some of my forces to round up Jonas. Thanks for the information, Temprus."

The City leader nodded and left police headquarters. He had done his duty as far as reporting to Chief Stapper was concerned. Now it was time to deal with his own civic duties.

As Temprus entered his own office, a familiar sound came. It was the trans-temporal communications device. He suspected who it would be on the other end.

CHAPTER 36

On a timeless plane, lack of empathy

"Why have you framed an innocent man for murder?" the Entity thought to Illyad.

Illyad pondered that question without replying at first. He had his reasons for what he had done and perhaps it was time to let the Entity know that.

"It was not to cause grief to Jonas," Illyad thought. *"It was for the greater good of ridding Valleria of a hated prostitute. When I had my own body, I carried out such cleansing on a regular basis."*

The Entity paused, then thought: *"And you are the final say – in your mind – of what the greater good is? Why not work with people who have fallen off the righteous path and instead help them, rather than destroy them?"*

"Too much work for too little gain. I prefer to work for the good of all Vallerians and I can't waste time on trash."

"Trash? You speak of people as if they were refuse."

"Some are."

"Your lack of empathy is displeasing," the Entity thought. *"What if someone with power over you labelled you as trash?"*

"I don't see that happening."

"It could."

"I don't believe that."

"We will meet again further, Illyad. For now, I return you to Valleria."

All went silent.

CHAPTER 37

Circa year 2150, reports coming in

Temprus appeared, fists clenched, in Dixon Slade's time. After talking to Slade via the trans-temporal communications device, Temprus thought it was time to go hunting for the person – or persons – who held a temporal signature that mirrored Illyad's.

Temprus had appeared close to Slade's headquarters and, after a brief walk and talk with the mechanical people at the headquarters, he was in front of Slade's door. It opened, revealing the Metropolis leader.

"Welcome, friend Temprus," Slade said as he motioned Temprus to enter his office. "I wish this meeting were under better circumstances."

"As do I, my friend. You said you have once again received reports of time travel activity in the 2350 era?"

"Yes. And it's becoming more prominent. I don't know about you, but it concerns me ... could it really be Illyad back from the dead?

"When it comes to the matter of my father, anything is possible." Temprus sat in one of the comfortable chairs in front of Slade's desk. "Yes, virtually anything."

"I agree. We in this era continue to track the temporal activity through the ages, but it does seem concentrated in the era 200 years hence. I fear Illyad – if that is indeed the person we're dealing with – has plans of his own for Valleria, as he had in the past."

"Well, when you're ready, we can take another trip into the future."

"I'm ready now. Let's go."

Temprus clenched his fists and the two men were whisked to 2350.

CHAPTER 38

Circa year 2350, Illyad's plans

Illyad/High Governor Morag sat at the head of the
Council of 11 table. The other governors had departed,
leaving the joined entity to ponder what had taken place.
Jackoo Governor Rollins had become quite heated
during the meeting, making further threats of war against
the absent Makown Governor Ting, who, for his part,
had sent the rest of the council a thought message
voicing his displeasure with the council in general and
Rollins in particular.

"Ah, this is going better than I had planned," Illyad said
out loud, with the Morag half of the joined persona in a
heavy slumber. "Perhaps I should send a message to
Ting, to stoke the fires of war all the moreso."

With that, Illyad sent a thought message to Ting,
describing in detail what Rollins had said about the
Makown governor. And Illyad embellished Rollins'
words, making them sound even more harsh than Rollins
had voiced. In the time zone of Makown it was night,

Illyad realized, and Ting was unlikely to get the message until morning.

"No matter," Illyad thought. *"I have plenty of time for warfare."*

The joined being sat back and relaxed. Illyad had planted as many seeds as possible to lead to war, for the time being at least, and now Illyad/Morag could attend to other, more mundane, duties of running their own continent of Vexall.

Illyad/Morag got up and walked out of the council chamber to their office. It was time for a drink from the newly-stocked bar that Illyad had had installed. He/she went to the bar, poured a shot, and downed it.

"Ah, this tastes almost as sweet as the meeting's outcome," the joined being said aloud before pouring a second shot and drinking it.

Then, a buzzer sounded, signalling guests. It would turn out these guests had come to 2350 from other times in the past.

The joined being ushered the visitors into his/her office.

CHAPTER 39

Circa year 2350, no answers

Temprus and Dixon Slade eyed High Governor Morag. Temprus couldn't quite describe it to himself, but there was something about her he didn't trust.

"Well, gentlemen, I don't know what to tell you about these temporal excursions you speak of. I've had no mention of them here," Illyad/Morag said.

"That's odd. We've seen a spike in activity emanating from this area," Slade replied. "It's odd indeed."

Illyad/Morag summoned refreshments for her guests – tea with herbs and spices – and they continued to talk. Ultimately, however, the guests were left with no answers.

"Well, High Governor, we'd like to stay in your time for a little while yet. Tell me, do they still have libraries in your era? I'd like to visit one if that's possible," Temprus said.

"Of course. I will send you the directions to the nearest one in a thought message. I'll also give you the instructions to mentally access our news feeds so you can keep up on things in our time," Illyad/Morag said.

The two men thanked their host, then made their way to the library. It was far different from what they were used to.

"Dixon, I just don't trust Morag. I think she's hiding something."

Slade looked at Temprus as the two sat down at a rather bare table in the library. "I agree. There are things here we aren't aware of. Let's get to those news feeds … perhaps we can find something going on in them."

The men concentrated, focusing inwardly on the news. Slowly, but surely, information began to make its way into their minds.

"This is interesting about this Ting character. It seems as if Valleria is on the brink of war with this man at the forefront of it," Temprus said.

"By the Source, I agree. Things look bleak for peace."

The two continued to mentally scan the news. Something might reveal itself … something that would confirm their fears about Morag.

CHAPTER 40

Circa year 2350, going to war

Makown Governor Ting had been awake for hours and had received the thought message from High Governor Morag (although Illyad had truly been the one who sent it). Ting was, to say the least, furious.

"Rollins is a complete bastard," Ting raged about the governor closest to him geographically. "If he wants war, he'll get it."

Previously, Ting had planned to consult with his Ministry of War to determine the best course of action. However, after that message – and the thought news feeds that he was monitoring, detailing Rollins' words regarding Ting after the latest Council of 11 meeting – the Makown governor decided consultations were not necessary. He would order a pre-emptive strike on the Jackoo continent.

Ting sent out a mental message to his generals. They were to prepare for war immediately. The continental

shield around Makown would go up as the first step –
just in case Rollins was ready for Ting's assault. Then,
the massive solar-powered ZX drones equipped with
xantha cannons (which would send out vibratory waves,
disrupting targets on a molecular level) would be
deployed. Those weapons would open holes in the
target's shield, allowing long-range artillery with xantha
technology to slip through. Troops – by air, water and
ultimately land - would follow once the shield was
down.

Ting smiled. It would be a quick war, he imagined, and
Jackoo would kneel to his will. If other continents
wanted to rush to Jackoo's defence, he would crush them
as well. After all, he reasoned, Makown was the largest
continent not only in terms of land mass but military
might as well.

Quickly, the generals relayed messages back to Ting.
As he expected, they were all in favour of a massive
assault on Jackoo. That was no surprise, as he chose the
most bloodthirsty people to lead his armies.

Soon, the war would begin. And Ting had no idea of just who was really behind it all.

CHAPTER 41

Circa year 2350, support for Jackoo

Jackoo Governor Rollins awoke just after midnight as the first artillery shells from Makown hit his continent's massive protective shield. The shield had snapped on just before the artillery fire was detected by Jackoo's defences, preventing the shells from causing any damage. However, the shield would not hold forever, Rollins knew, and action had to be taken immediately.

"That bastard Ting," Rollins said as he jumped out of bed, knowing intuitively that the Makown governor was behind the attack. It could be no one else, Rollins thought.

Rollins began sending out thought messages to his generals, preparing them to launch a counteroffensive. Since Jackoo had been in a state of alert for some time, it would not take the Jackoo military long to spring into action. Even so, Makown's armed forces were generally regarded to be the most powerful among Valleria's 11 continents and Rollins knew he would have to ask for help from the other governors. The first step in that process would be to contact High Governor Morag and Rollins quickly sent a thought message to her.

Halfway around Valleria, Illyad/Morag received the message. The joined entity grinned in Illyad's typical fashion.

"Ah, the word that I had been waiting for," Illyad/Morag said. "Ting has played the cards of war just as I hoped he would."

The joined being replied to the message, promising aid from not only the head Vexall continent but others as well. The other governors disliked Ting but they might fear his military power. A balanced effort, with Makown eventually being weakened just enough by the other continents' efforts, would open the door for Illyad to take over Makown – and, later, the rest of the continents as well.

Illyad/Morag stood in the joined being's office and began sending out thought messages to the other governors. As the joined being suspected, not all the other governors were eager to take on Ting. However, several continental leaders voiced support for Jackoo and vowed they would join in on the effort to defeat Ting's forces.

The war was on. Illyad/Morag grinned again.

CHAPTER 42

Circa year 2350, seeking information

Temprus and Dixon Slade were continuing to monitor the thought news feeds at the library when all kinds of mental reports came flooding in about the attack on the Jackoo continent. It seemed unreal … this era had seemed relatively peaceful up until now.

"By the Source, this is terrible," Temprus said. "With the weaponry available in this time, millions – nay, billions – could perish."

Slade looked grim as he took in the news feeds. There was a deluge of information available about the attack, none of it good, he noted.

"Temprus, this situation reeks of Illyad. I don't know if we can do anything to stop this new war but, if there is a possibility of ending it, we must track down Illyad – if, indeed, he is behind this."

"I agree. Perhaps we should continue to scan for information on Morag ... I believe the answer lies with her."

"Yes, I agree. Let's put the feeds on the conflict aside for the moment and continue to look into any news about her."

Both men sat still for a moment, then went back to the feeds about Morag. Their search for information on her might take some time – the information feeds were vast – but it was their best hope in putting an end to the war – if anyone could.

CHAPTER 43

Circa year 2350, hero in the making?

Illyad/High Governor Morag sat behind the joined entity's desk and grinned.

"So, the war continues," Illyad thought. *"Good. That fool Ting played this out just as I planned."*

However, Illyad continued, it had best be good – at least for appearances – that High Governor Morag be concerned about these most recent developments. *"I had best send out another thought message to the governors – including Ting – calling for an end to hostilities."*

So, scant minutes later, the message went out. Illyad knew Ting would disregard it… and as for the other governors, who cared what they would do? Some might yet come to Rollins' defence, others not. But really, who cared? Certainly not Illyad.

"I will let these idiots play out their little war. And when they have beaten each other into submission, who

will come forward to save the day? Myself, of course ...
or, as they will see it, Morag."

Illyad/Morag rose from the desk and went to the
recently well-stocked bar – a bar Illyad had filled to his
own specifications. He chose a particularly strong liquor,
poured a shot, and downed it. Then another. And
another.

"This is a day that will go down in Valleria's history.
And I – or Morag – will eventually look like the hero."
Illyad drank again and grinned.

CHAPTER 44

Circa year 2350, shelling the transportation grid

Makown Governor Ting watched the viewscreens in what he had now dubbed his war room (formerly his office). He was pleased to watch the artillery shells coming from his continent crashing into the shield of Jackoo.

"Eventually that shield will collapse," Ting said aloud with glee. "Rollins and his continent will fall." It didn't escape him that his own shield would soon be taxed with incoming weapons fire from Jackoo and, perhaps, other continents. But how best to prevent that incoming fire from coming about? He couldn't do much about Jackoo's weapons, at least for the moment until that continent's shield went down, but perhaps he could hinder other continents from joining in. How best to do that? By disrupting – or outright destroying – the transportation grid joining the various continents of Valleria. He called his aides and instructed them to contact his generals.

"Yes, if the grid is destroyed, we – I – will reign supreme over Jackoo and, eventually, the other continents," Ting laughed.

Scant minutes later, the first of the generals contacted Ting, who gave him his marching orders. The other generals soon called in and Ting told them what he wanted done.

Within the hour, the shelling on Jackoo stopped. But it wasn't because of a cessation of hostilities. The weapons of Makown were redirected at the grid.

And then, Makown's weaponry opened fire once again.

Almost immediately, the grid surrounding Jackoo was hit again and again with shell after shell. The modified wormhole transportation tubes exploded, one after another.

Jackoo Governor Rollins, hopeful after the bombardment had ceased on his continent's shield, looked with alarm at what was happening to the surrounding transportation grid. Jackoo would be completely cut off from the other continents in short order. He knew that would make it more difficult to get aid from his neighbouring leaders.

"Damn," Rollins said to himself. "We'll be on our own shortly."

That was precisely what Ting had planned.

CHAPTER 45

Circa year 2350, frustration

Temprus and Dixon Slade, at the library, continued to scan the news feeds for information about High Governor Morag. Although there were some interesting facts here and there, ultimately there was nothing concrete that would implicate her in the new warfare going on throughout Valleria.

"By the Source, this is frustrating," Temprus said to Slade. "With the technology available to us, you would think something of use would come up about this woman."

"You're right," Slade replied. "We're coming up with nothing on her."

For a time, the two men carried on their information search on Morag. They wound up with little of any use. However, reports began to pour in that Makown Governor Ting's forces had, for the most part, destroyed the planet's transportation grid. Where before travel between the continents was possible within minutes, now – with the grid out of the picture – it could take days or even weeks to get from one continent to another, depending on the mode of transportation.

"Friend Temprus, I believe it is imperative that we make our way to Ting to try to stop this madness. He is, aside from Morag, the key to ending this."

"I agree, Dixon. But first, I must travel to my own time for a brief period … there is a murder investigation I must check in on."

"Very well. I should also tend to matters in my own time, for an equally brief period. And when my work there is complete, we must carry out our mission to contact Ting."

Temprus nodded and Slade returned it. With that, Temprus clenched his fists and whisked the two men back into the past, each to his respective time periods. The war would have to wait for a short time until they returned to 2350.

CHAPTER 46

Circa year 1950, heavy slumber

Temprus appeared in his own time after delivering Dixon Slade to 2150. He was determined that his stop here would be short … granted, he had a murder investigation here in 1950 that needed his attention, but all-out war was escalating in the future.

Police Chief Stapper was waiting for Temprus at police headquarters.

"Temprus, what say you about your trip into the recent past? Anything more?"

"No, chief. But Jonas was definitely with Trina on the night of her death."

Stapper allowed himself a grim smile. Up to now, he had nothing concrete to point to anyone in the murder. Now, he had a positive identification that would lead to an arrest.

"Thank you, Temprus. My detectives and I will be making our way to Jonas' residence in short order."

With that, Stapper called on two of his best men and updated them on this development in the murder investigation. The three of them left headquarters and made their way to Jonas' residence. Stapper knocked on the door and got no response. He tried the door and, to his surprise, he found it unlocked.

Inside, the three of them searched the residence. Ultimately, they found Jonas in a heavy slumber. It was so deep that their attempts to wake him were unsuccessful.

"We'll arrange for an ambulance to pick him up and take him to a guarded hospital ward," Stapper told his men. One of the men left to make the call, then returned to wait with the others until the ambulance arrived.

"This is strange," Stapper told his men. "Stay with him at all times."

With that, Stapper left to inform Temprus of what he had found.

CHAPTER 47

Circa year 2150, passionate kisses

Dixon Slade walked into his office after being dropped off in his own time by Temprus. Previously, he had been raring to go to prepare for the upcoming council meeting, and the talk that would ensue about the trans-temporal program, but he found his heart and mind weren't in it now.

First, his thoughts went to his wife, Melissa. He found he couldn't stop thinking about her and how he had neglected her in recent times due to the ongoing matters in the various eras. And he was also thinking about the conflict in 2350 … would he and Temprus be able to help there? Slade couldn't say.

But, for now, he would concentrate on his wife. He couldn't stomach the thought that he wasn't including her in his life. Slade sat down behind his desk and called her.

'Hello, sweetheart," Slade began. "I love you."

"And I love you ... I haven't heard from you for a while. Is everything all right?"

"There is plenty to tell you, and I'd like to tell you, over a meal. Are you available now?"

"My work for today is compete. Do you want to meet at our usual restaurant?"

"Certainly, dear. I will meet you there in an hour."

Then, Slade quickly tended to some civic matters before making his way to the restaurant. Melissa was already seated at their favourite table. Slade sat down after giving Melissa a passionate kiss and they looked into each other's eyes, deeply, the way they used to.

"Dixon, tell me what's happening. You're definitely not yourself."

From there, Slade told his wife all that was happening in the future era. Her eyes widened as he spoke.

"Dixon, I believe you and Temprus have to follow your hearts to help the people of the future. Please, please, just be careful."

"I will, my dear. Thank you for understanding."

They dined, laughed a bit, and shared a glass of wine. Then, it was time to depart. They had another passionate kiss and then Slade left to go back to his office, where he would call Temprus on his trans-temporal communications device.

It was time to return to 2350.

CHAPTER 48

Circa year 2350, viewing the destruction

Illyad had left High Governor Morag's body behind, in a coma-like state, in her quarters. He wanted to see firsthand the destruction that had been wrought by Makown Governor Ting.

Illyad's essence rose from Morag and sped to the Makown continent. He didn't need the transportation grid for the trip – his essence could travel at incredible speeds and the journey to Makown from the Mega-opolis took him scant seconds.

"Excellent," Illyad thought as he saw the barrage between Makown and its neighbouring continents. The war had started between Makown and the Jackoo continent initially, but Governor Ting had diverted some of his firepower to the transportation grid that had connected not only Jackoo but other neighbouring continents. In response, those continents had opened fire on Makown's shield and its part of the grid. Makown, and the other continents, were effectively cut off from

each other save for water ships that could pass through the shields with special codes. As for air and space travel, it had been discontinued due to the danger the ongoing war presented to airborne craft.

The massive weapons of the continents continued to fire. The shields of those continents were powerful beyond words but, in time, even they would collapse and let the weapons do their work on the lands of Makown, Jackoo and the other players in this war.

Just then, Illyad felt ... *something*. It took him some time to figure out just what that was.

Then, it came to him. Another time traveller was entering this era.

"Temprus. Welcome, son," Illyad thought.

CHAPTER 49

Circa year 2350, an older method

Temprus, fists clenched, arrived in 2350 Mega-opolis with Dixon Slade. They had already thought about their first steps in this future era and they included going to the library to catch up on events.

After a short walk, they arrived at the library and began to access the thought information feeds available there. They were shocked.

"By the Source," Temprus said to Slade, "most – if not all – of the transportation grid is destroyed. How will we get to the Makown continent to stop Ting's rampage?"

Slade thought for a moment. "Let's access alternate modes of inter-continental transportation."

The two put their thoughts to the task, finding that airborne modes of transport were out of the question. So were most others methods of transportation.

"There's got to be something," Slade said. "Let's keep searching."

Both men pored their minds through the vast archives of information available. Eventually, they found some old-style fishing boats that might be available.

"Excellent," Temprus said. "They might not be the best method of getting to Makown but they're better than nothing."

"Agreed. Let's try contacting some of these boat owners and see if any of them is brave enough to try to get through to Makown."

From there, the pair started sending out thought messages in the hope that someone would reply. They would have to wait and see.

CHAPTER 50

On a timeless plane, mayhem and suffering

The Entity drew Illyad's essence to a timeless place where they could commune.

"It was already awful, what you did with Jonas," the Entity thought. *"But what you have now done to Valleria – initiating full-scale war – is unthinkable."*

Illyad paused. Then he thought back.

"What I have done is for the greater good. Eventually, this war – which will end at some point – will leave me in power over Valleria. The planet will reap untold rewards by following my commands. Technological advancement ... social benefits ... a time of untold peace and prosperity will follow."

"That is what you think. What if you are wrong ... and at what cost will these benefits come with? Untold billions could die."

"It is a high price, I admit. But a price well worth it. In the end, you will see I'm correct."

"I will see no such thing. All that will come from this is mayhem and suffering."

Illyad paused but he was resolute. He was determined to see his plan of action come to fruition.

The Entity thought again.

"If my rules of non-interference were different, I would stop you. You deserve nothing but pain for what you have done."

"Ah, but your own rules prevent you from stopping me. I will rule supreme over Valleria, eventually."

The Entity was silent, pondering what had transpired. And Illyad returned to the war-torn planet that was under his grip.

CHAPTER 51

Circa year 2350, peace be damned

Makown Governor Ting was in a deep slumber –
something that was rare since the war had started – in
which he dreamed of a disastrous defeat for his
continent. He awoke soaked in sweat. Ting had always
believed in the power of dreams, in their ability to
foretell the future, and he thought he must take action to
prevent that vision from coming true.

"I cannot lose … I cannot …" Ting mouthed aloud.
Even though it was the middle of the night, Ting got out
of his bed, dressed, and made his way to his war room.
There, he went over various thought reports that told the
tale of his self-made war. With other continents joining
in against Makown – particularly since Ting had fired on
the planet's transportation grid – there was a danger that
Makown could go down to defeat.

"NO!" Ting yelled, knocking items off his desk. "This
must not be!"

There was only one thing to do, Ting thought to himself. Escalate the war.

So, Ting called his generals and admirals from their respective sleeps and ordered them to meet him in short order. He only gave them scant minutes to do so.

When the leaders of his forces arrived, Ting was brief.

"I want Jackoo to be a smoking crater, to instill fear in the other continents. Deploy all of our fleet against Jackoo," Ting told them.

Some of the assembled war leaders, already uncomfortable with how things had gone thus far, were inwardly nervous about these new orders. But they knew those who disagreed with Ting tended to … *disappear* … so it was best for them not to voice dissent.

So, the war would escalate. And peace be damned.

CHAPTER 52

Circa year 2350, ready to go

It was over an hour since Dixon Slade and Temprus, still at the library, had started sending out thought messages to the captains of several fishing boats. They had yet to receive a reply. It appeared the mission to Makown was too dangerous for most of these captains to undertake.

Then, when they had all but given up hope, one of the captains – concerned for the future of Valleria, and who wanted the war stopped at any price – replied that he would take the pair to Makown.

"By the Source, this is good news. I was beginning to think we'd have to swim there," Slade said to his companion.

"Good news to be sure," Temprus replied. "But how do we get to the fishing boat? It's far away from Mega-opolis proper."

The two thought for a few moments, then Slade spoke. "The android Circuit-5 … if we can contact her, she could take us to the vessel. I wonder if she can receive our thought messages?"

"Let's try." Temprus concentrated and sent a message to the android. To his mix of astonishment and good feeling, the android responded and said she would be able to pick up the two men in a short period of time.

"Excellent," Slade said. "She should be here shortly."

True to her thoughts, Circuit-5 walked into the library in a brief time.

"Good day, gentlemen. Can I give you transportation?" she asked.

"Yes, please," Temprus replied. "Do you know where we're headed?"

"Yes," she said. "The coordinates were in your thought message. Are you gentlemen ready to go? The transport craft is just outside the library."

With that, the three of them left the library, boarded the craft and departed. Time was of the essence.

CHAPTER 53

Circa year 2350, dangerous mission

Rango, captain of the fishing boat *Wasser*, stood on the deck of his boat and waited for the arrival of Dixon Slade and Temprus. He knew nothing of these men other than what was in their thought messages, but they seemed sincere – and maybe a bit foolish – in their desire to stop the war.

"What a mess, this damn war," Rango said aloud as he began pacing the deck. "They're making this planet a shambles." He continued some boatkeeping duties, plotting a course to Makown and looking after the rigging of the craft. It hadn't changed much over the years, this wood and metal boat, and it was still as sturdy as the day it was launched.

Just as Rango was beginning to wonder if his guests would arrive, on the horizon he spotted three figures coming his way. "It must be them."

Minutes later, the trio of figures touched down in front of the boat. Temprus and Slade thanked Circuit-5, who left on the transport craft.

"Allow me to introduce ourselves, captain. I'm Dixon Slade and this is my friend, Temprus,"

"Welcome, boys," Rango said to the two men. With his long, white beard and salt and pepper hair going down around his dark orange skin, Rango could get away with calling grown men 'boys.'

"You know from our messages what we are looking to do," Temprus said. "What say you, Rango, about our mission?"

"It's dangerous beyond words, to be sure, but I've never been one to play it safe. I love an adventure, even one with as much potential peril as this. For our voyage, we'll have to cross the largest ocean on Valleria, and that comes with dangers of its own, let alone all the weapons fire going on."

"By the Source, you're right,' Slade said, before asking Rango if they needed any supplies. Rango replied, saying all the things they would need were already on the boat.

"Climb on board, boys, and let's be off," Rango said with more than a hint of gusto. As he had said, he loved adventures … even ones that he wasn't guaranteed to come back from.

CHAPTER 54

Circa year 2350, a common enemy

Illyad awoke in High Governor Morag's body. He wanted a drink to celebrate the ongoing war that, in his view, would lead to a united Valleria ... united in a way never before seen.

As the joined being went to the bar in Morag's quarters, Illyad began accessing the planetary information feeds via Morag's brain. The news continued to be good – at least in Illyad's estimation. The conflict was escalating.

"That fool Ting," Illyad thought. *"He's playing right into my plans. Nothing unites people like a common enemy and that is precisely what Ting has become."*

Illyad thought he – or, more to the point, Morag – should send some moral support to Jackoo Governor Rollins. Several other continents continued to support Jackoo but the military might of the Makown continent was not to be underestimated. Ting might yet win the war.

"No matter," Illyad thought within the confines of Morag's brain. *"Whether Ting wins or not is irrelevant. I*

will take over the victor and, in so doing, take over the entire planet."

Illyad crafted a thought message to Rollins to express the support of the Council of 11 (minus Ting, of course). Vexall and the other continents would support Jackoo (although it was of little consequence since Vexall had little in the ways of weaponry, even though it was equipped with a high-level defence shield).

Then, Illyad began searching the news feeds again. Would there be any word on a time traveller from another era? Illyad wondered what his son was doing in this era.

"Temprus ... we're so different, and yet in some ways, so alike," Illyad thought.

CHAPTER 55

Circa year 1950, a presence

Police Chief Stapper eyed Jonas as armed guards stood by in the City Hospital room. The prime suspect in Trina's murder had awakened about an hour ago and Stapper was ready to ask him some questions.

"Where were you when Trina was murdered? We have a witness who places you at the scene of the crime not long before her death."

Jonas' mouth opened as he searched for words.

"I swear to you, I don't know what happened. I was … walking … in the streets … and that's the last thing I remember. I swear to you, I don't know what happened."

"That's convenient," Stapper replied. "You'll have to come up with a better story than that, Jonas."

Jonas, his right wrist handcuffed to his bed, sought words again.

"The last thing I remember before waking up in this hospital bed was … *something* … near me. It was the strangest sensation. It was like something was … taking me over …"

"A likely story. And, again, convenient."

"I swear to you I didn't kill anyone!" Jonas exclaimed. "There was a … *presence* … something that seemed to come nearer and nearer to me. I don't even remember this Trina woman … I don't know what happened to her!"

Stapper turned to the armed guards.

"Keep close watch on him," Stapper said. "I'll be at headquarters if something new arises, or if Jonas changes his story."

With that, Stapper left, pondering the words that Jonas had spoken to him.

CHAPTER 56

Circa year 2350, rough around the edges

Captain Rango looked out from the *Wasser*'s deck. The wind was favourable today - a good day to embark on a lengthy voyage.

The captain's guests on this excursion were helping out at much as they could before they embarked. These two were land lovers, Rango noted to himself, and he would end up doing the Arkor's share of the work.

"Oh well," the captain thought to himself, *"it is for a good cause. The best of causes, in fact… saving the planet from this evil man of Makown."*

Time passed as the three of these new boatmates prepared for the voyage. The only fishing they would be doing would be to feed themselves on the way – although there were plenty of provisions on board – so not all the fishing equipment needed to be deployed, making for a quicker start.

"You two, look lively," the captain said to Temprus and Dixon Slade as the latter two took a break from preparations. "We'll never get underway if the two of you dawdle along."

"Aye captain," Temprus said with a smile. This Rango character was a little rough around the edges, Temprus noted, but he was growing to like the captain nonetheless.

A couple of hours later, preparations were complete. It was time to get going on their quest to Makown.

None of the three knew what awaited them on their voyage.

CHAPTER 57

Circa year 2350, blow them to hell

Makown Governor Ting read the latest reports coming in to his command centre. There was increasing firepower coming in to Makown's shielding – not just from Jackoo, but from neighbouring continents that had come to Jackoo's aid.

He was enraged.

"So, they think they can beat me, eh?" Ting yelled out to no one in particular. "I will show them who is in charge."

Ting immediately set up a thought conference with his generals and admirals, ordering additional strikes against the other continents. The transportation network had already been effectively destroyed, so he ordered strikes against their shield generators – if he were able to destroy them, the other continents would fall in short order.

"Yes, blow them to hell," Ting thought to his military leaders.

From there, those leaders went on to further the attacks. Ting was confident he would be victorious.

But then …

A little bit of doubt entered his mind.

Had he taken on more than even he could handle? No, Ting dismissed the idea.

He would be victorious in the end, he thought to himself.

CHAPTER 58

Circa year 2350, planning a ceasefire

Illyad, having left High Governor Morag's body behind in a state of coma, departed for Makown at a speed only his essence could muster. He wanted to see firsthand the damage to Makown's shield due to the ongoing onslaught from the other continents.

At length, and a short length at that, Illyad arrived in the skies above Makown. He marvelled at how well the mammoth shield of the continent had withstood the firepower of its neighbours.

"Even so, the shield can't last forever," Illyad thought to himself. *"Perhaps I can arrange for a ceasefire, even if it's a temporary one, to give it a chance to recharge."*

Shell after shell hit the shield as Illyad looked on. Eventually, he thought, it would be time to return to Morag's body to work on the ceasefire.

It was time for that, Illyad reasoned. His essence moved high above the carnage that Makown had become and surveyed, again, the destruction he had wrought.

"It's a shame it had to come to this but it's necessary for the greater good," Illyad thought. *"The more this plays out, the better it will be."*

Illyad pondered the ongoing onslaught, then turned his attention to the ceasefire he had deemed necessary. His essence began moving at lightning speed back to the Mega-opolis. He returned to Morag's office and began planning the ceasefire.

CHAPTER 59

Circa year 2350, sea creature

Temprus and Dixon Slade stood at the starboard side of Captain Rango's fishing vessel, looking out over the open sea. They were silent as the vessel made good time on the voyage to Makown.

"By the Source, the spray from the salt water makes me feel good," Temprus said to Slade. "How about you?"

"I agree. Things seem to be going in our favour thus far."

Just as the two seemed content to watch the sea waves going by them, Rango yelled out: "Sea creature off the port bow! Prepare the harpoons!"

Temprus and Slade rushed to the other side of the vessel and saw an enormous kroockrus, a huge, six-tentacled monster, not too far away. The kroockrus moved its tentacles menacingly in their direction as it made its way towards the trio.

"Fire the harpoons!" Rango yelled out.

Two harpoons launched from the bow of the vessel. One was a clear miss, the other hit one of the tentacles, causing the creature to bellow in pain.

Then, Temprus clenched his fists and directed his temporal powers at the kroockrus, causing it to slow to a stop. Having lost its momentum, the creature sank into the sea.

"You'll have to show me how to do that trick some time," Slade smiled at Temprus.

With the crisis averted, the *Wasser* continued on its way. More perils no doubt lay ahead.

CHAPTER 60

Circa year 2350, eager for peace

Illyad, in High Governor Morag's body, sent out a thought message to the Council of 11. Even Makown Governor Ting was included.

"It is time for hostilities to cease," the thought message said. *"Please, come to your senses."*

The message went on to call for a meeting of the council in the Mega-opolis. There was no time to lose, it continued, as Valleria was getting closer and closer to planetary annihilation.

"That fool Ting won't go for it, but it will cause the other continental leaders to pause," Illyad thought to himself.

The hours ticked by and the news feeds showed no letup in the firepower being directed from and toward Makown. Finally, to Illyad's surprise, the weaponry ceased firing on both sides.

"What is Ting up to?" Illyad wondered.

Then, to Illyad's further surprise, a thought message came in from Ting himself.

"High Governor, I agree that we must cease hostilities. However, how can I trust the others – and especially Governor Rollins – that we won't be under attack once more? Things have gone on too far."

"Good," Illyad thought to himself. *"Ting is playing at peacemaker. This will have an interesting conclusion.'*

Now, how to play this out, Illyad wondered. Then it came to him.

"We will have a thought conference, Ting, let me arrange it with the other governors," Illyad – through Morag – thought messaged Ting.

The other governors would be eager for peace, Illyad thought to himself. As for what Ting wanted – well, that was yet to be seen.

CHAPTER 61

Circa year 1950, hoping for headway

Police Chief Stapper sat at his desk at police headquarters, pondering his time with Jonas. The prisoner was under guard, and would remain so for the foreseeable future. What Jonas had said about being taken over by ... *something* ... continued to churn in Stapper's mind.

"What if he's telling the truth?" Stapper wondered. *"But that's impossible ... isn't it?"*

Stapper continued to go over his staff's reports on Trina's murder. Jonas was placed at the scene of the crime shortly beforehand, of that there was no doubt. It wasn't an ironclad case, to be sure, but Jonas was by far the most likely – and at this point, only – suspect.

Stapper continued to mull over the reports, thinking again and again that there must be something that he and his team were missing. He couldn't help but wish he could get in contact with Temprus ... there was something about Jonas' words that made Stapper think that Temprus could be of great help right about now.

But getting in touch with Temprus now wasn't possible, as the City leader had left word that he would be unavailable for some time.

So, that left this case up to Stapper and his team.

The chief decided to call his staff working on this case together. Perhaps if they shared their thoughts, they could get somewhere.

At least, that was Stapper's hope.

Over the intercom, Stapper called his secretary. He instructed her to gather his team.

Stapper hoped that, together, they could make headway on the Jonas case.

CHAPTER 62

Circa year 2350, pirates!

Temprus and Dixon Slade stood near the bow of the *Wasser*, contemplating their mission. It had been days since their encounter with the six-tentacled creature and they were relieved that their trip had been uneventful since then.

However, their relief was to be short-lived.

As the *Wasser* cut through the salt water en route to Makown, with Captain Rango at the helm, Slade and Temprus thought they would make use of their time by taking up some fishing. They broke out the rods and reels and started to cast. Soon enough, some fish were biting.

"Ah, this is the life, eh?" Slade asked Temprus.

"Aye, that it is."

Then, on the far horizon, the three men saw a larger vessel. It slowly drew closer and Rango gasped in alarm.

"Boys, that's a pirate ship! I thought those buggers were extinct but I guess they've been revived in these here parts!"

Rango pushed his relatively smaller vessel to its limit, trying to escape the pirates, but his engine was no match for theirs. They drew closer and opened fire on the *Wasser*. Rango did his best to move away from them but, despite his efforts, they continued to draw closer.

"Can't you do something?" Slade asked Temprus. "The pirate vessel is out of range of my telekinesis."

"Soon … they are also out of range of my temporal powers. Be patient."

The pirate vessel drew closer … closer … and then, at last, they were in range of Temprus' powers. He clenched his fists and the pirate vessel stopped dead.

Once again, the *Wasser* and its crew were safe. The journey to Makown continued.

CHAPTER 63

Circa year 2350, planning an attack

Makown Governor Ting sat back in his comfortable
chair. He laughed to himself, pondering the upcoming
thought conference.

"The fools," Ting thought. *"They will play right into
my hands ... I will make them believe I am seeking
peace, and when their defences are down, I will destroy
them."*

It would be some time before the conference, so Ting
thought it was an opportune occasion to take a stroll in
his garden. It was the best place to come up with plans
for the destruction of his adversaries, he reasoned, so
why not mix business with pleasure?

"See to it my guards are on hand in the garden," he told
one of his quivering underlings. She nodded and hurried
away quickly, the better to be away from Ting.

Minutes later, Ting was strolling in the garden, with the
guards a respectable distance behind him. He smiled as

the Source shone down on him and the trees surrounded him. He walked for a while before sitting down on a brightly-coloured bench beneath a central tree.

"Ah, this is grand, much like myself," Ting said aloud.

But, the time for work was at hand. He planned to destroy Rollins' continent first, of course, and that could be done by his naval forces – as long as they were in place when the time was right. However, he had to be careful not to forewarn Rollins so his defences weren't up when Ting's navy attacked.

"Yes, this will take some planning," Ting said.

The governor got up from the bench and continued walking to his war room. The day would come when Makown would reign supreme on Valleria, Ting vowed to himself.

CHAPTER 64

Circa year 1950, brainstorming

Police Chief Stapper paused over the steaming cup of coffee he had placed on the long, wooden table in front of him. The other half-dozen people seated at the table in City police headquarters did the same over their beverages,

Then, Stapper spoke.

"People, we need more evidence in this murder investigation. True, we do have a suspect, but the case against him is flimsy at best."

At Stapper's right, Deputy Chief Haugen shifted his position in his chair. Haugen didn't like mysteries, particularly ones in which people died. Then, he spoke.

"We're already combing the area and questioning the neighbours," Haugen said. "Perhaps it's time we changed our tactics, chief."

"What do you mean?"

"To be truthful, I'm not entirely sure. But I am certain there is something more to this murder than we have seen so far."

Stapper looked around the table at the other members of his investigative team.

"Do the rest of you have any ideas? Let's brainstorm this."

For the next hour, those at the table bounced around ideas on how to proceed. For the most part, they drew blanks. However, some ideas did draw the chief's attention, including checking more thoroughly into the suspect's past.

Eventually, Stapper stood up and addressed the group.

"Well, we've made some progress here. Let's get out there and solve this case. Dismissed."

CHAPTER 65

Circa year 2350, arriving at Makown

The *Wasser* approached a relatively unguarded section of Makown's southern coast. Captain Rango brought his vessel to a halt and let loose his anchor.

"Well, boys, this is it. I will wait here for you as long as I'm able, assuming a bunch of bloody troops don't come out of hiding and open fire on me. You can take the rowboat the last bit of the way."

"Thank you, captain," Dixon Slade said, with Temprus nodding in agreement. "How can we repay you?"

"By stopping this Ting bastard. That'll be payment enough."

Slade and Temprus launched the rowboat and made their way for the beach. Just beyond that the vast shield blocked their entry to the rest of Makown, but the two of them had a theory about getting past that barrier.

"Temprus, as we discussed before, our powers – used in tandem against the shield – might just punch a hole in it big enough for us to get through."

"I hope we're right, or we might as well get used to relaxing on the beach while Ting destroys half the planet."

They reached the beach and pulled the rowboat on dry land. Then, the two of them prepared themselves to use their powers to the utmost against the shield.

But would this work? They would soon find out.

CHAPTER 66

Circa year 2350, don't trust him

Illyad, in the body of High Governor Morag, pondered just how the upcoming thought conference would go. It was mere minutes away and Illyad wanted to make sure things went according to his plans.

"Ting is an idiot," Illyad thought. *"He has played right into my hands. However, he does command the mightiest military force on the planet ... he is playing at peacemaker now but I don't trust him. Perhaps I should bring his main adversary, Governor Rollins, into my web."*

With that, Illyad/Morag sent a thought message to Rollins of Jackoo, outlining the sense of mistrust the joined being (although Rollins thought it was just Morag's message) had when it came to Ting.

"I wouldn't trust him," the message read. *"Keep your guard up regardless of what Ting says. He is a liar."*

For his part, Rollins was somewhat surprised at the message even though he agreed with it. He didn't trust Ting but thought Morag would play this war game with more diplomacy.

"I don't get her. She asked for a halt to hostilities and yet sends me this message. Strange," Rollins thought. He was a reflective man and the message gave him reason to pause.

Meanwhile, half a world away, Illyad/Morag grinned. Ting would continue to be the common enemy in this equation. With any luck, Ting would fall to the other continents and Illyad would solidify his power through Morag.

He/she grinned again, flexed his/her powerful female muscles and waited for the thought conference to begin.

CHAPTER 67

Circa year 2350, taxing their powers

Temprus and Dixon Slade stood on the beach on Makown's southernmost shore, facing the massive shield that surrounded the continent. Each braced himself for what was to come next.

"Prepare yourself, Dixon. Let me know when you are ready."

"Aye, Temprus. This will tax our powers like never before."

The two stood side-by-side, each raising his fists to focus the power within them. Slade gritted his teeth while Temprus' clenched fists glowed golden with temporal power.

"Go!" they yelled in unison, unleashing their telekinetic and temporal abilities at a single spot on the shield.

For what seemed like an eternity, nothing happened. Then, slowly, plumes of smoke began to emanate from the shimmering barrier.

"Pour it on!" Temprus exclaimed at his comrade, who yelled in response.

Temprus' power was making the shield section age while, at the same time, Slade's telekinesis was bending it inward. Sparks showered from that part of the barrier.

Then, at last, the section collapsed in a heap of fire and energy. They could see clearly through the other side and both men ran through the hole in the shield, lest it repair itself immediately.

They were on the other side of the barrier. They had made great progress in their quest, but plenty of work – and a long path – lay ahead.

CHAPTER 68

Circa year 2350, working for peace

Illyad/High Governor Morag sat back in his/her comfortable chair at the head of the Council of 11 table. Even though the other governors weren't physically here, the thought conference involving all of them was beginning.

"Greetings, all," the joined being thought. *"Welcome."*

"Let's get on with it, please," Makown Governor Ting thought. *"I have pressing matters on my continent to attend to."*

The other governors were surprised at Ting's use of the word 'please' as this was highly out of character for him. Was he on the ropes, so to speak, in the war that had been suspended for the time being? They would see.

"I, too, have other matters to look after, but this is of the utmost importance," Jackoo Governor Rollins thought. *"I'm sure the rest of us can say the same."*

The governors exchanged pleasantries before getting on to other issues and, eventually, to the heart of the matter – the suspended war.

"How can I trust that you'll honour the ceasefire, Rollins?" Ting thought.

"Me? How about you? You initiated this conflict."

Illyad/Morag interceded.

"Gentleman, please, this is getting us nowhere. Let's all agree in principle to keep the war abated and work for peace."

The governors agreed to that. And Illyad/Morag grinned as the conference came to a close.

CHAPTER 69

Circa year 2350, strangers

Dixon Slade and Temprus stood on Makown soil and took a look at their surroundings. They were on the inside of the massive shield, which still had a small hole in it.

"Well, we're inside. Now we must make our way to Ting's headquarters and see what can be done there," Slade said.

"By the Source, this won't be easy. But our way so far hasn't been a smooth road either," Temprus replied. "We'll find a way."

"Transportation won't be an issue. I can move us over the land with my telekinesis," Slade said. "Let's be on our way."

Slade concentrated and the two men were lifted two metres off the ground through his power. He gently moved them forward, slowly at first, then with more speed.

"We're in farm country now but I'm sure we'll find some main roads soon," Temprus said.

Soon, they came across a farm house. And there was a couple outside of it and they were praying.

"Let's stop here," Slade said. "We can ask for directions and talk with these people."

Slade gently brought himself and Temprus to a halt on the ground and the two of them approached the couple.

"Greetings," Temprus said. "We are strangers here."

The couple eyed them and smiled. "Welcome to Makown," the man said. "I am Metrus and this is my wife, Marita. Please, come inside." The four of them made their way inside the farm house and prepared to talk.

CHAPTER 70

Circa year 2350, plotting

Makown Governor Ting sat in his war room, contemplating just how long he would continue with the charade of the ceasefire. His monitors were focused on the Jackoo continent, and he was waiting to see if Governor Rollins would make the first move.

"That coward Rollins," Ting said aloud. "He doesn't have the guts to attack again."

Meanwhile, Rollins was in his own control centre, wondering what Ting was up to. Rollins definitely didn't trust the head of Makown by any stretch.

"Unless I miss my guess, weapons fire will start at any time," Rollins thought. *"We'll keep the shield up in case anything changes."*

Rollins continued to eye his own monitors, waiting for any action on Ting's part. This was a nerve-wracking game, Rollins thought, and could go on for days or even weeks. Just how long it would last would be up to Ting.

"I might as well get some sleep," Rollins said as he watched the chronometers on his console. It was late, and besides, if weapons fire did break out, he would be alerted and out of bed in short order.

Rollins slept as Ting continued plotting. For once, the Jackoo governor would get a good night's sleep.

That's not to say the next night would be the same.

CHAPTER 71

Circa year 2350, a place to stay

Metrus and Marita prepared a meal and set the kitchen table for themselves as well as Dixon Slade and Temprus. After the meal was ready, the four of them sat at the table.

"Let us pray for this meal," Marita said. The four of them prayed.

After that, Slade asked: "To whom are you praying?"

"The Redeemer. The Saviour of Souls," Metrus replied.

Slade and Temprus looked at each other. "We, too, believe in a higher power," Temprus said.

"Many of our people do. It's all the more important since Governor Ting came into power on Makown," Marita said.

Slade turned his gaze on a large clock on the far wall. "Why do you say that?" he asked.

"Why, Ting is evil. He doesn't care about his people," Metrus replied.

The four of them continued to eat the meal, the aroma of which filled the kitchen. They could hear the patter of rain on the rooftop.

"You are welcome to stay the night. We can build a fire to keep warm," Marita said.

Temprus and Slade nodded in unison.

CHAPTER 72

Circa years 2350/1950, unwitting victim

Illyad left High Governor Morag's body in a comatose state once again. He had a mild interest in what was happening to Jonas back in 1950 and his essence time-travelled several hundred years to the past.

"Ah, poor Jonas. An unwitting victim of my whims," Illyad thought as his essence arrived in the 1950 City.

His essence – invisible to the citizens of the City – scouted out various spots, looking for Jonas, until at last Illyad found him. Jonas was still in handcuffs.

"Jonas ... poor Jonas," Illyad thought to himself.

Illyad took some time from the victimized Jonas to look around the City. It had, indeed, grown since he ruled there and he was pleased with that.

"Of course, it would have grown more with me in charge," Illyad thought. *"But I have other opportunities for myself in the future. I had best get back there."*

Once again, Illyad travelled the centuries, this time headed for 2350 and Morag's body. His essence entered her frame and the joined being awoke.

"Yes, time for my plans to come to fruition in this era," Illyad/Morag said.

CHAPTER 73

On a timeless plane, secrecy

"Greetings, Illyad," the Entity thought.

"I was just in Morag's body ... why have you brought me here?"

"I was displeased with your interaction with Jonas. He is a mere pawn in your game."

"He is an unfortunate casualty, I agree. But little can be done."

"I disagree," the Entity thought. *"You can reveal yourself to the authorities."*

"Why would I do that? Secrecy is key to what I am doing."

The Entity paused, then thought again.

"Secrecy is cowardice. Only by being transparent can you attain a true goal."

"Now, I disagree. I must be left to pursue my goals as I see fit."

"No. But I return you now to Valleria," the Entity thought.

Illyad awoke again in Morag's body.

CHAPTER 74

Circa year 2350, careful eyes

After leaving the home of Metrus and Marita, and following a good night's sleep and a hearty breakfast, Dixon Slade and Temprus viewed the surroundings with careful eyes. They had received directions to Makown Governor Ting's headquarters and were determined to head that way. With his telekinesis, Slade again lifted the pair off the ground and moved them in Ting's direction.

"Even at the speed we're going, it will take some time," Slade cautioned his comrade. "You might as well enjoy the ride."

"Aye, I will. The countryside of Makown is beautiful, isn't it?"

"Yes, I agree."

The two made their way over hilly terrain until, at last, they came upon one of the main roads of Makown. This road would eventually lead them to their goal, although it was still some time away.

"We had best stay a bit off the main path, lest someone report two flying men on the roadway," Slade said.

"Of course, you are correct."

The two were well off the roadway as they made their way toward Ting's headquarters. They would have time to think about what they would do once they got there.

CHAPTER 75

Circa year 2350, memories

Makown Governor Ting, having awoken to a beautiful day, decided to spend it in his garden. After a sumptuous breakfast – made, as always, just to his liking lest he be displeased with his chef – he and two heavily armed security guards made their way outside.

"Ah, glorious," Ting muttered aloud. The fragrance of the flowers always made him go into a relatively good mood.

Ting walked the paths of the garden flanked by his guards. He couldn't remember the last time he walked freely without them. It must have been in his father's time. That thought made him pause and sit on a bench in the garden's centre.

"Father," Ting thought. *"Why couldn't you have seen things my way? It was time for me to come to power all those years ago. If you simply had abdicated, I wouldn't have had to have you assassinated."*

It had been some time since Ting thought of his long-deceased father. He still had mixed feelings about his parent ... part of him missed his father (in spite of the way he died) while the bigger part of him relished the power the man's death had brought him.

With that, Ting got up and commenced walking once more. The guards followed on either side.

He made his way to the memorial to his father in the garden, where his ashes remained buried. Ting paused at the sacred spot and mouthed a silent prayer.

Then, Ting returned to his war room. There was other business to attend to.

CHAPTER 76

Circa year 2350, solidifying power

After awakening in High Governor Morag's body, Illyad decided to go over his plans for this era. Things had slowed down drastically since the ceasefire, and he decided it was time that he took advantage of that.

"It's time to solidify my power here," Illyad thought. *"And I can do that by taking credit for the ceasefire."*

The best way to do that, Illyad reasoned, was by letting the planet's news outlets know that Morag had brokered this fragile peace. In addition, he would also let it be known that Makown Governor Ting had started the war. So, the joined being sent out a carefully crafted thought release to those outlets outlining the details – as Illyad crafted them – of the warfare and subsequent ceasefire.

In the release. Illyad brought all the credit for the ceasefire to Morag's doorstep and damned Ting as the architect behind the war. It was all too easy to make the Makown governor look like the scapegoat.

"Ah, glorious," Illyad thought. *"Unless I miss my guess, this will prompt Ting to reinitiate the war."*

Illyad wasn't far off the mark. Nearly instantaneously, Valleria's news outlets began circulating the release and reaction to it.

Soon, the war would start anew.

CHAPTER 77

Circa year 2350, no time to lose

Dixon Slade and Temprus, metres off the ground and suspended by Slade's telekinesis, continued on a speedy path to Makown Governor Ting's headquarters. It was a bright day, with the Source shining down on them as they made their way over the terrain of Ting's continent.

"What say you we stop up ahead at that pond?" Slade asked his comrade. "I could use the rest."

"Excellent idea, my friend," Temprus replied.

As the two approached the pond, Slade slowed them down somewhat. He had been moving them quickly across the land and he was feeling fatigued. He set them down on a sandy spot by the edge of the water.

"Ah, it looks like there are some fruit trees just over here," Temprus said, pointing. "Let me get us some food."

The two ate the fruit Temprus had picked from the bottom branches of one of the trees and they relished the sweet taste. However, their rest was to be broken soon after as the sound of massive weapons fire came to them from a distant location.

"Oh, no. The war must have resumed," Temprus said. "After we rest, we must waste no time in getting to Ting." Slade nodded in agreement … there was no time to lose.

CHAPTER 78

Circa year 2350, ceasefire ends

"Hehhehheh," Makown Governor Ting giggled as
Xantha weaponry crashed into Jackoo's shield. It had
been mere minutes since the barrage had restarted,
ending the ceasefire, but Ting relished the explosions
nonetheless.

"So, Morag thought she would blame me for the war,
did she?" Ting yelled aloud as the barrage continued.
"She'll live to regret sending out that thought release."

For his part, Jackoo Governor Rollins had begun to
return fire and his own Xantha weapons smashed into
Makown's shield. He shook his head from his own
vantage point, pondering why High Governor Morag had
sent out that release.

"That was foolish," Rollins said aloud. "This just
prompted Ting to restart the war."

Ting continued to cackle to himself, before sending out
a thought message of his own to his military brass. He

wanted his troops at the ready in case Jackoo's shield eventually collapsed. That was unlikely to happen anytime soon, but still, it paid to be prepared to invade the neighbouring continent when the time came.

And halfway around Valleria, Illyad grinned with Morag's mouth. This had worked out just as he had hoped.

CHAPTER 79

Circa year 1950, spotless reputation

Deputy Chief Haugen sat at his desk, reviewing his team's investigation into Jonas' history. The team had conducted interviews with numerous City citizens as well as gone to Jonas' home territory, talking to his family and friends.

As of yet, nothing had turned up to suggest Jonas had the makings of a killer. Far from it – Jonas had a near spotless reputation.

"I wonder if there is anything we're missing," Haugen wondered aloud. Could there be some unknown chain of events that the team had overlooked?

Haugen decided to bring the team's findings – or lack thereof – to Chief Stapper's attention. Haugen left his office and made his way to the chief's and knocked on the door.

"Enter, please," the chief said from inside. Haugen entered, with a grim look on his face.

"It looks like you've had better days," the chief said. "What is the problem?"

Haugen took a seat in front of Stapper's desk.

"Well, chief, so far, Jonas is coming out spotless. Not a mark on him."

Stapper frowned. He had been certain something would turn up in Jonas' past to explain the murder.

The two men would later see there wasn't.

CHAPTER 80

Circa year 2350, bombardment

Illyad had just left High Governor Morag's body in a comatose state in her quarters to make his way to the Makown continent to see how the war there was progressing. Not much to his surprise, he found several other continents had joined in with Jackoo in firing upon Makown.

"Excellent," Illyad thought to himself. *"This is going just as a planned ... that fool Ting will fall, he will become the target of blame for all this, and Morag's – my – power will be solidified."*

For a time, Illyad watched as shell after shell from the other continents bombarded the Makown shield. Just how long the shield would hold was up for debate. What was not up for debate was that it would fall, eventually, and Ting would be forced to surrender. For Makown's part, it was firing back at a rapid pace, with most of its long-range artillery focused on Jackoo.

"Enough of this observation," Illyad thought. *"It's time to return to Morag."*

Illyad's essence began travelling back to Morag's body at a dazzling rate. Illyad himself was amazed at the speed he could muster.

At last, Illyad was back in Morag's quarters and within her body.

Illyad/Morag awoke.

CHAPTER 81

Circa year 2350, on the horizon

Temprus and Dixon Slade resumed their journey to Makown's capital city, held aloft by the latter's telekinesis. It was a speedy trip and they expected to make their way to their destination in short order.

"By the Source, I can't understand the foolishness of this war," Temprus said to his comrade. "What can Ting hope to accomplish?"

"I know not," Slade replied. "All I know is we have to do what it takes to stop it."

They carried on their trip, with various craft in the air in the distance. It was a sign they were getting closer to the capital. To their right, a small city was visible and it connected to the capital via various networks.

"Ah, there are people all around us now. We must be getting closer," Temprus said.

"I agree," Slade said.

The pair carried on past the small city and through the meandering countryside. Then, along the horizon, they saw gleaming towers far off.

They would soon be at Makown's capital.

CHAPTER 82

Circa year 2350, propaganda

Illyad, in High Governor Morag's body, was indeed pleased at how the war was turning out. Governor Ting was sure to fall, but he wanted to add some insurance to make sure that happened.

"That fool Ting," Illyad thought. *"It would be best if he were out of the way in short order."*

Illyad sent out another thought message to the continental governors, insinuating further that Ting was responsible for the war. Of course, the governors had seen Ting all but destroy the transportation network of Valleria earlier, so they were eager to believe just about any anti-Ting propaganda that Illyad (through Morag) could muster.

"Ting must be stopped at all costs," the thought message read. "The very future of Valleria depends on it."

And with that thought message, the remaining continents that had been staying out of the conflict began to rally their forces. They, too, would soon attack Ting.

Hours passed, and then, increasing weaponry was aimed at Makown's shield. Shell after shell – thanks to Valleria's high-level artillery technology – smashed into the shield.

"They are all fools," Illyad thought, grinning inwardly.

CHAPTER 83

Circa year 2350, nagging thought

Makown Governor Ting sat in his command centre, viewing report after report of the increasing barrage against his continent's protective shield.

"Damn that Morag," Ting thought. *"She has everyone involved in the war now."*

Up to now, Ting was confident that the neighbouring Jackoo continent would fall before Makown's arsenal. But now, things were different.

"What if I lose?" Ting thought. For the first time, he considered the proposition of defeat and what that would mean for his regime – and himself, personally.

Ting turned his thoughts toward another front. He would go down fighting regardless of the odds against him. He didn't think of the people of Makown and that he would be leading them into an increasingly hopeless cause.

"I can't lose ... I can't," Ting thought to himself.

Still, in the back of his mind, a nagging thought persisted in Ting's consciousness.

What if he did lose?

CHAPTER 84

Circa year 2350, capital city

Dixon Slade gently let himself and Temprus down on the roadway leading into Makown's capital city. The city looked massive, with all kinds of craft in the air circling it.

"I'm surprised we haven't been met with an armed contingent," Slade said. "This Ting character seems like the type to encircle his city with thugs of all sorts."

"I imagine his headquarters will be heavily fortified, however," Temprus replied. "We'll see what happens when we get closer to it."

The pair walked without incident into the city and marvelled at the architecture. Huge towers were on either side of them They approached a citizen and asked where Ting's headquarters could be found.

"Oh, it's in the centre of the city," the citizen replied. "But I'm not sure you want to go there." He pointed in the direction of the headquarters.

"Thank you," Temprus said. "We'll be on our way."

The visitors from the past continued walking in the direction the citizen had pointed to. There was nothing to do now but make their way as best they could.

The headquarters awaited them.

CHAPTER 85

Circa year 2350, the only option

Makown Governor Ting sat in his headquarters, watching the ongoing escalation of hostilities against his continent unfold. With the incoming Xantha shells coming in from just about every direction, now that all the other continents had joined in on the attack on Makown, he feared it was only a matter of time before Makown's shield collapsed.

"This cannot be," Ting thought. *"I am destined to be the leader of Valleria."*

But, increasingly, it didn't look that way. Bit by bit, parts of the shield were showing signs of strain.

Ting sent out a thought message to his military leaders. He wanted them to be prepared for, what, more and more, seemed inevitable. The thought message outlined terms of Makown's surrender, if it came to that.

The leaders messaged back, with some expressing the opinion that it would be better to die fighting than surrender. Others accepted the terms without question.

As for Ting, he sat back in his high-backed chair and continued to watch shell after shell smash into the shield. His heart beat more loudly in his chest as some of the shells finally made their way through, exploding on Makown soil.

Surrender was the only option.

CHAPTER 86

Circa year 2350, coming into power

Illyad/High Governor Morag sat in the Council of 11 chambers, monitoring the news feeds. It appeared inevitable that Governor Ting would fall to defeat, considering the awesome barrage pounding Makown's shield.

"Nothing like a common enemy to unite a people," the joined being said aloud. "Once Ting loses to the other continents, my power – through Morag – will be solidified."

One part of the common victory bothered Illyad. No one would know it was him who actually was in power. *"Regardless ... it will be I who is in command,"* Illyad thought.

Illyad began plotting his next moves. Once Ting was defeated, the transportation grid would have to be rebuilt, as a start. The war had, indeed, taken its toll. And a meeting of the continental governors – minus Ting, of course – would have to be convened to figure out war reparations. Ting's continent would have to bear the brunt of the costs of rebuilding the grid, plus covering any other damages the planet had suffered as a result of the war.

But, one thing was certain. Illyad would be in charge of Valleria, even if nobody on the planet except for him knew it.

Illyad, with Morag's mouth, grinned.

CHAPTER 87

Circa year 2350, surprise to come

Dixon Slade and Temprus approached Makown Governor Ting's headquarters, with – surprisingly – not much in the way of opposition. Little did they know that Ting's security forces were concentrated within the headquarters, close to the governor himself.

However, a massive wall surrounded the headquarters itself. Temprus and Slade eyed the wall and then looked at each other.

"My friend, I think we'll get past this wall the same way we got through the shield," Temprus said.

"Agreed," Slade replied.

The pair concentrated their time travel and telekinetic powers at a single spot on the wall. Compared to the shield, the wall collapsed fairly easily.

When the section of wall opened up to reveal the gardens beyond, Slade and Temprus stepped inside, prepared for anything. And anything happened – several security guards came running in their direction, and Slade – with his telekinesis – knocked them out.

"I'm sure we'll find more guards," Slade said, adding: "Let's go find Ting."

The two of them continued the search within the walls of the headquarters, and soon came to the heavy doors leading to Ting's war room. They would be surprised at what they would find.

CHAPTER 88

Circa year 2350, surrender

Illyad, in High Governor Morag's body, grinned.

"Ting's shield is collapsing. I believe his mind will soon collapse as well," Illyad thought.

The former dictator continued to monitor the thought feeds as they came in with increasing speed. Indeed, the Makown shield was letting in shell after shell.

"It is time to end this. It is time for Ting to surrender and die," Illyad thought.

Illyad left Morag's form in a comatose state and began the journey to Makown. With incredible speed, Illyad was at Makown in mere minutes.

"Ah, here I go into the headquarters," Illyad thought. Once inside, Illyad viewed Ting, sobbing, seated in his war room. Then, Illyad entered Ting's body. Once there, he crafted a thought message that would make it clear to

all the other governors and news feeds: Ting would surrender.

A short time later, the barrage on Makown stopped. And the war ended with it.

Now, Illyad thought, how to do away with Ting. Poison? A knife?

"I believe the latter will do," Illyad grinned with Ting's mouth.

CHAPTER 89

Circa year 2350, startling

Dixon Slade and Temprus stood in front of the heavy doors leading into Makown Governor Ting's war room. Alarms continued to sound throughout the area, but to their surprise, no additional guards were in sight.

"No guards … perhaps they've abandoned their leader in this time of crisis," Slade said, and Temprus nodded.

Then, the two of them turned their attention to the doors. Getting past them would require all their combined powers. They looked at each other, then the doors. Then, they concentrated their special abilities on this final barrier.

Minutes passed and, finally, the doors began to buckle. Eventually, they collapsed.

"Be prepared for anything," Temprus said. "Indeed," Slade replied.

They walked through the remains of the doors, alert for any and all opposition they might find. They found none.

What they did find, however, was startling.

Ting sat in his command chair, surrounded by flickering viewscreens. And in his left hand he held the handle of a large knife … and the blade was plunged deep in his heart.

"Ting is dead by his own hand," Temprus said.

And a familiar grin was etched into Ting's mouth.

CHAPTER 90

Circa year 2350, dreams of conquest

Illyad went, once again, into the comatose body of
High Governor Morag. Then, he looked around, using
her eyes.

"Ah, this is the dawning of a brave, new day for
Valleria," Illyad/Morag said.

The first thing to do was heal the hurting from the war
… and solidify Illyad's power base, of course. The
joined being sent out a thought message to the
continental governors, to set up a group thought meeting.

And the purpose of the meeting? The joined being
hadn't put that in the message in so many words … but it
was to move most of the power of the planet into the
office of the high governor.

"Then I can dominate as I see fit," Illyad thought.

The joined being went to the well-stocked bar that the
former dictator – and, in his mind, future dictator – had

installed in Morag's quarters and poured a drink. Illyad/Morag downed one drink, then another. Eventually, they went to sleep.

And inside Morag's mind, Illyad dreamed of the conquests to come.

CHAPTER 91

Circa year 2350, strange feeling

Temprus, with Dixon Slade behind him, approached Makown Governor Ting's dead body.

"By the Source, I'm sensing something," Temprus said. "I hadn't had this feeling before arriving at Makown."

Slade put a thoughtful look on his face.

"Perhaps it's the extent you ... we ... have used our powers since arriving at this continent. We've definitely stretched our abilities beyond the point that we've been used to."

"Agreed," Temprus replied. "And, now, I can sense temporal energy in this place and on Ting's body in particular."

"What is it? What do you sense?"

"It's hard to put into words. It's like an echo from another person ... another being."

Temprus put his hands on Ting's cold shoulders. And then, he backed away.

Slade looked alarmed.

"Temprus, what is it? What do you sense?"

Temprus paused and then spoke.

"It's Illyad. My father was here, in Ting."

CHAPTER 92

Circa year 2350, a proposal

Illyad, in High Governor Morag's body, awoke in time for the thought meeting among the governors. He was looking forward to this meeting.

"Ah, the fools will surrender their power to me without knowing it," Illyad thought. *"It is only a matter of time before I take total control of Valleria."*

The joined being sat at the head of the Council of 11 chambers, relishing in the feel of planetary conquest. True, many had died in Illyad's quest for power – not only from the constant shelling, but from riots involving factions for and against the war on various continents – but many more would benefit from his rule, Illyad reasoned.

Soon, the governors began to mentally check in to the meeting. Jackoo Governor Rollins was the first to put his thoughts in – not to Illyad's surprise.

"That coward Ting is dead at last," Rollins thought. *"By the Source, I'm not sorry to see him go."*

Illyad agreed mentally, as did most of the other governors. Eventually, after some more mundane thought conversation, Illyad came to the point – his point – of the meeting.

"Friends, we must prevent such a war from ever happening again. This is what I propose to ensure that," Illyad thought through Morag's mind.

The other governors went silent, at first not believing what they had heard. What Morag (truly Illyad) was suggesting that the power of the planet be completely concentrated in the office of the high governor. The Council of 11 would be redundant and a showpiece only.

And Illyad, with Morag's mouth, grinned.

CHAPTER 93

Circa year 2350, not beyond belief

Temprus and Dixon Slade had made the journey back to Captain Rango and the *Wasser* and the three of them were en route once more to the Mega-opolis. They didn't have to worry about shelling this time around, however.

On the front deck of the *Wasser*, Slade and Temprus were having a conversation regarding the late Governor Ting.

"Temprus, I'm perplexed about the finding you made on Ting. It seems incredible … that Illyad had the power to somehow physically control Ting."

"It's more than that, Dixon. I sensed that … somehow … Illyad, or what's left of him, entered Ting and took control of him. I believe Illyad entered Ting's body and, after controlling it, killed him."

"Incredible. But really, when it comes to Illyad, nothing seems beyond belief."

"I agree. And I also think that we must confront Illyad and stop him before he does more harm."

"No doubt that is true. But where will we find him?" Slade asked.

"If Illyad were to inhabit another body, whose do you think he would take over?"

Both men paused for a moment, then spoke the answer aloud: "Morag's."

And on the *Wasser*'s front deck, the two men prepared to confront a being who had likely become more powerful than ever.

CHAPTER 94

Circa year 2350, blinding light

At the Mega-opolis headquarters of the Council of 11, Illyad/High Governor Morag awaited Temprus and Dixon Slade. The two had thought messaged their arrival ahead of time.

However, the joined being did not expect the two to come armed with Temprus' new ability to detect Illyad's presence. The doors to the Council of 11 chambers opened and in walked the men from the past.

"Greetings," Illyad/Morag grinned, thinking of their coming dominance over Valleria. *"There will be some changes, to be sure,"* they continued grinning.

Temprus and Slade looked at each other … that was the signal, to confirm Illyad's existence, they had planned for.

"Father," Temprus said simply. "It has been a while."

Illyad/Morag stopped grinning, and the joined being crossed his/her arms in front of their chest.

"So, you've found me out, son. Your ingenuity makes me proud."

Temprus frowned.

"Unless I miss my guess, you're behind all this warfare Vallerians have had to suffer through in recent times. It has your trademark on it. Why?"

"For the greater good, of course. I'm not the evil being you've made me out to be. Many had to die so more could live prosperous lives."

"Under your rule, of course?" Slade asked.

"Under my guidance, Slade," the joined being replied. "People who don't deserve to live – like that prostitute back in my son's time – should be exterminated so others can excel."

"So, it was you who killed Trina. I should have known," Temprus said, adding, "you realize we'll have to stop you, father."

"How? I've become more like a god than I ever have been, son." And the joined being grinned again.

With that, a blinding white light filled the room and the joined being collapsed. Slade and Temprus rushed forward.

Morag opened her eyes, alone, for the first time in a long time.

"What has happened? Who are you two men?"

Temprus detected no presence of Illyad. He nodded at Slade with a sigh of relief.

"High Governor Morag," Slade said at length, "we have a story to tell you."

CHAPTER 95

Circa year 2150, friendship

Dixon Slade and Temprus arrived in Slade's time,
coming from 200 years distant after explaining things to
High Governor Morag. She had her work cut out for her,
looking after the post-war 2350.

As for the two friends, they each had responsibilities in
their respective times. They both believed they had
ignored matters in their own eras for too long. As they
arrived in Slade's office, the two men smiled and
breathed deeply … it had been some time since they had
the chance to relax.

"Friend Dixon, you must be eager to spend some time
with your wife. I don't blame you."

"Aye, friend Temprus, it is high time we had a romantic
dinner together. And I've got to deal with Curtis Trelane
and the rest of my council when it comes to the temporal
program. More than ever, I'm convinced it must
continue."

"I wholeheartedly agree. In this instance, defeating
Illyad depended on it."

"I concur. Can I interest you in a drink before you head back to your own era?"

Temprus smiled and nodded, and the two sat at either side of Slade's desk after he poured a couple of drinks. They clinked glasses and drank heartily.

For the two of them, it was an all-too brief time of friendship before Temprus returned to 1950.

CHAPTER 96

Circa year 1950, peaceful times

As if from nowhere – it had been some time – Temprus walked into Police Chief Stapper's office.

"Temprus! Just when I had thought I would never see you again, you're back! What stories do you have to tell?"

"Plenty, chief. I was in the future and … well … it might take a while to fill you in. But more importantly, how have things been going in the City?"

"As well as ever, I suppose. Our investigation into the Trina murder has had some stumbling blocks, but we continue to hold Jonas as our main suspect."

That made Temprus pause and scratch his chin. Then, he spoke.

"Ah, yes, Jonas. Probably the most important thing I have to say to you from my journeys in the future is I uncovered the real killer, complete with confession."

"Really? That's amazing! Who is the killer?"

"My father, Illyad."

"Illyad? But the word on the street is that he was killed long ago. How can he be the murderer?"

"With Illyad, it appears just about anything is possible. But trust me, he is the killer. However, he's taken care of, I believe. We won't be bothered by him again, if my suspicions are correct. Please, see to it that Jonas is released, with the City's apologies."

"If you say so, Temprus. Right away."

With that, Temprus walked out into the City streets. The Source shone down from above and Temprus was looking forward to a peaceful day.

CHAPTER 97

On a timeless plane, taking action

"Greetings, Illyad. I trust you are well," the Entity thought.

"What have you done? I feel strange."

"Responding to prayers from the people of Valleria, I have decided to take action ... an action that is a first in my existence. I have made a minor adjustment to the planet's magnetic field. The change is undetectable by most, but if you stay on Valleria for more than just a few minutes, it will prove fatal to you."

Illyad's essence sank.

"You spoke of non-interference! This goes against that!"

"Ah, Illyad, you have gone much too far. That explains why I took this step. And I didn't do this without consulting a higher power. You see, even I have to answer to that power. Think of me as the ... caretaker of Valleria in the broader universe."

"But what of me?"

"Ah, Illyad, the universe is vast and I can't speak to all of it. All that matters to me is the welfare of Valleria and

its inhabitants. As for you, you are banished from the planet for all time. Farewell."

EPILOGUE

I am Illyad.

My essence can no longer exist on Valleria, due to the change in the magnetic field. No one on the planet would notice the change but it means my home planet is no longer my home for me.

I am Illyad.

It has been centuries since I have been on Valleria. My essence makes its way through the cosmos and I look for other ways to gain power. Other worlds are ripe for the taking.

I am Illyad.

On other planets I have become known by many names. On one I am Feldikar, on another I am Jenikan while on others, I am simply known as the Devil.

Take your pick.

THE END